VOL. 4, NO. 4

ISSUE #16

FEATURES

NEW STORIES

FROM THE CAT'S PERCH

I never thought much about what constituted a historical mystery until I moderated "Groovy Kind of Death: Murders Set in the '60s/'70s," a panel at Bouchercon Minneapolis in 2022, and realized I was leading a discussion about historical mysteries set *during my lifetime.*

That was an eye-opener.

When I was born, the US had only forty-eight states, and many significant events have occurred since then. This was made clear to me a few years earlier when, as an adult attending university later in life, most of what we studied in US Constitution felt like current events to me but not to my much-younger fellow students.

For this special issue, we explore historical mysteries, and contributors take you to Germany, Paris, Venice, and various locations in the US. The events of many stories occur in the first half of the 20th Century, but Elizabeth Zelvin takes readers even further back.

Though Mr. Peabody and Sherman aren't with us (a historical reference fans of "Peabody's Improbable History" should catch), step into the Wayback Machine by turning the page and diving into crimes of the past.

* * * *

Stories from *Black Cat Mystery Magazine* continue to be recognized, and 2024 was no exception.

"Real Courage" by Barb Goffman (*BCMM* 14) was nominated for Agatha, Anthony, and Macavity Awards, and "El Paso Heat" by Peter W.J. Hayes (*BCMM* 14) was selected for inclusion in *The Best Mystery Stories of the Year 2024.*

—Michael Bracken
Editor, *Black Cat Mystery Magazine*

Staff

PUBLISHER & EXECUTIVE EDITOR
John Gregory Betancourt

EDITOR
Michael Bracken

WILDSIDE PRESS SUBSCRIPTION SERVICES
Karl Wurf

PRODUCTION TEAM
Sam Hogan
Karl Würf

MASTERPIECE
MARK THIELMAN

Dots of paint, nothing more, yet they captivated him. Philippe looked again at the small painting, *Young Girl with a Straw Broom*, the title plate said. She had a cherubic face, round and full. Rembrandt had smudged her cheeks with dirt. In the chiaroscuro of the background, her brown, tattered dress blended with the wall behind her, the lines separating building and cloth subtle and indistinct. From this palette of shadows and darkness emerged her face, like the full moon shining over the Seine on a dark night. Her wide eyes, brown with flecks of gold, pierced him. They seemed to see into Philippe's soul. Looking at her, he saw an angel who had flown too close to the ground.

Perhaps, he thought, he saw the children of Paris. Since the occupation, life had been hard for everyone, with food and fuel shortages, and soap in short supply. Dirty children whose faces knew too much about life, sadly proved common.

He heard the click of approaching boots across the parquet floor of the Jeu de Paume. Philippe quickly dropped the canvas covering the painting. Snatching the broom he'd leaned against the wall, he swept at the floor, resuming his janitorial duties.

The overweight man in the elaborate uniform marched past him. "Where is the director?" Feeling the twist in his stomach, Philippe slowly looked up from the square of tile he'd been studying.

"He is not here, Herr Reichsmarschall," the director's secretary, a thin woman in a tweed suit said, emerging from the uniformed entourage following the Reichsmarschall. "He has gone to inventory the most recent collection of seized paintings."

Philippe dared a glance. Hermann Goering, Hitler's second in command, stood in profile to him. He had overfed jowls and a thick brow. Peeking out from this cave of fat were small, beady eyes. How differently he carried a chubby face than *Young Girl with a Straw Broom*, Philippe thought. After the momentary peek at the enemy, he dropped his gaze to the floor.

"You there," Goering barked in his direction.

Philippe lifted his head slightly. "*Oui*, Herr Reichsmarschall?"

The outstretched arm pointed at the broom. "Keep the dirt from here. I do not want to see my paintings damaged."

Philippe bobbed his head. "*Oui*, Herr Reichsmarschall."

Goering's head snapped back toward the secretary. "I will be back in three weeks. Have a courier deliver the inventory to my curator. He will tell you what paintings to have on display. Then I will decide which shall be transferred to Waldhof Carinhall."

"*Oui*, Herr Reichsmarschall."

He marched past, instantly oblivious to their presence, his aides in fawning pursuit. The secretary grabbed Philippe's sleeve and pulled him into the director's office. Opening a desk drawer, she withdrew a bottle of brandy and two small glasses. Hand trembling, she poured them both a drink.

"To that man's early death," she said and touched glasses with Philippe.

"Who is Waldhof Carinhall?"

She shuddered slightly. "Waldhoff Carinhall is his private art museum, outside Berlin. He stocks it with whatever he loots throughout Europe." Her shoulders shook again, and she quickly tossed back the remainder of her brandy.

* * * *

"I must save her from that beast," Philippe said back in his apartment.

"That is not the girl you wish to save," his companion tapped his forehead. "Asher here knows the girl you truly dream of rescuing."

Philippe's face flamed. "How many times must I tell you? Never call yourself Asher. Philippe, always Philippe. If you forget even once when the Boche are watching, they will capture you. Do you know what happens to Jews who fall to the Nazis?" Despite his obvious anger, he kept his voice to a whisper.

Asher, who, although taller with long, gangly limbs, bore a resemblance to Philippe, nodded. "*Oui, mon ami.*"

The two had become friends at the Ecole de Beaux-Arts in the pre-war days when Paris had been alive with artists. Asher's family had fled the Jewish Quarter of the 4th Arrondissement for the safety of the countryside. He had stayed to defend his city. After the fall of Paris, Philippe persuaded him to move into Philippe's small apartment above the Boulangerie Leon in the Rive Gauche. They lived as one person. If Asher ventured out, it was only at night, traveling upon Philippe's papers. The identity photograph did not show the height disparity between the two men. He always returned before curfew.

Asher straightened his arm and pointed to the mantle above the cold fireplace. "That is the girl you try to save, *mon ami.*"

Philippe collected the single candle they burned and studied the painting. In the flame's small circle of light, it was a study in shadows. The painting contained some of his best brushstrokes. He had painted her with a confidence he only occasionally felt. Clarice's eyes looked back at him as only his baby sister could. His was the first of many hearts she would stab, if… His mind would not allow the thought to continue. He prayed Clarice and their mother were safe in Vichy.

He returned the candle to the small table. "I want to save them both, Philippe." He placed special emphasis on the name.

Asher smiled. "As one Philippe to another, tell me. Why don't you just steal the painting?"

"You've not seen them. Nazis inventory their bowel movements. They catalog every painting there. If one is missing, they will know. They will line up the director and his secretary and start shooting until someone confesses."

Asher nodded. "Then they cannot know."

* * * *

Philippe awoke, the noise from the crowd gathering outside the Boulangerie Leon as effective as any rooster. The line formed early, people hoping to purchase a baguette before the baker sold out each morning. The racks emptied quickly on the limited flour ration. Still, the oven ran each day, warming Philippe's floor. He dressed barefoot.

He bicycled to work on threadbare tires, wending through the streets crowded with other bicyclists, pedestrians, and horse-drawn carts. Only the Nazis had petrol.

After he crossed over the Seine, Philippe pedaled by the burned remains of the synagogue. He passed the bonfire the Nazis seemed to keep perpetually going, into which they threw art and literature they deemed decadent. Into the flames, they threw anything Jewish they did not steal for themselves. Ironic that this spot was the only illumination in the City of Light. He pumped his legs faster to get away. Soon he came to the Tuileries; ahead was his museum.

Inside the Jeu de Paume, the director walked the galleries, his eyes downcast. At the sound of Philippe's footsteps, he looked up with alarm. Seeing Philippe, his face relaxed. The director pointed to the blank spaces on the walls. "Your work may soon hang here, Philippe. We may have nothing else to display."

Philippe raised his broom. "I have brought the wrong brush."

The director smiled, then his face broke and he turned.

Not wanting to embarrass his boss, Philippe quietly stepped away. He stopped in front of *Young Girl with a Straw Broom*. Standing to the right of center, he noticed for the first time, the red on her hands. A child's skin chapped from her labors. Every time he saw her, he discovered something fresh. He looked again at her enigmatic expression. Like Clarice, she knew things she would not tell him.

The director joined him, silently standing shoulder to shoulder with him.

"The painting is so small," Philippe said. "Don't you think the Nazis will want the big pictures?"

"Many confuse size with artistic merit." The director said before shaking his head. "But they are not fools. He brings a curator with him." He pointed to the bottom corner of the painting. "And the name. Everyone knows Rembrandt. Do not allow yourself the luxury of hope." He shuffled off, blowing his nose into a soiled handkerchief.

* * * *

On the ride home, a plan formed inside Philippe's head. The director's words had given him the idea. Philippe took the stairs two at a time. Asher turned to him, already wearing his coat. He moved to the door.

Philippe barred his exit. "I am sorry, but I must go out again."

"I've been trapped here for hours."

Philippe nodded. "I have an errand only I can perform."

Before Asher could object, Philippe dashed out the door.

Even in wartime, small art galleries still clustered around the Sacre Coeur. Philippe knew he must hurry if he was to make it to the Montmartre and return home before curfew. He silenced the inner voice telling him to rush. Carefully he studied the pictures available. He did not concern himself with the content. The size of the picture mattered along with the frame. The painting must be old, two hundred years at least. A Nazi may not know a Rembrandt from a Raphael, but he would recognize a shiny new nail. A simple frame devoid of gilt surrounded *Young Girl with a Straw Broom*. That made things easier. Old canvas in an old frame, these were his demands.

He found the picture he needed in the third shop. The painting, a commonplace landscape, was created by an artist no one remembered. The dealer knew Philippe, yet he acted as though he were being asked to part with his child. Philippe traded his father's pocket watch, a marvelous timepiece set in a gold case. The dealer grumbled but accepted; gold proved easier to carry than worthless paintings.

Asher laughed when he saw the painting. "This was your errand? I could have created better art with fireplace ash."

"You may get the chance," Philippe said. He outlined his plan.

"You want to forge a Rembrandt? It is madness."

"The fat Nazi comes to the Jeu De Paume expecting to see a Rembrandt. We'll show him a Rembrandt. I have watched them. It is like watching people shop in the market before the war. Their eyes race across all the paintings. They snatch one, or two, or ten. They do not stop to let the art seize their heart. This is not love, this is lust. And if his eyes skip over this painting, if he does not take it, then I shall return the original after he is gone."

"You cannot save all the art, Philippe. It is a fool's errand."

"I cannot save all the Jews either."

Asher said nothing.

Philippe put his arm around his friend. "It is only a drop. But if every

French citizen contributed a single drop, we could fill a very large bucket."

Asher looked from his friend to the canvas. "At least this fool's errand will give me something to do. A man could go crazy locked up in here."

* * * *

The next day they began. Philippe spent his free minutes at the Jeu De Paume studying the painting, memorizing the colors and the brushstrokes. Asher, meanwhile, scraped the landscape free from the canvas. Chips and flecks of dried paint fell to the floor, small bits of color piled like autumn leaves. He rubbed the canvas with a rag dipped in solvent, wiping away two hundred years of art. Asher worked slowly; solvents, like paints, were in short supply. He took care not to damage the aged canvas.

* * * *

"You're late," Asher said when Philippe entered.

"A crowd at the bonfire. The Boche pillaged a library of decadent literature. I had—" Philippe stopped midsentence. He noticed the twinkle in Asher's expression. "You have news?"

Asher shifted his gaze. On the table sat a small easel covered with a towel.

Philippe peeled back the covering. He stared at the blank canvas. "*Magnifique.*"

Asher nodded. "I hope you have studied your model."

The two began working immediately. They built layers of paint on the canvas, a base of white followed by a coating of brown.

Philippe looked at their dwindling supply of paint. "We must have enough."

Asher did not say a word. Putting on his coat, he collected Philippe's identity papers, a palette knife, and his rucksack.

Philippe glanced at his watch. "Curfew," he whispered.

Wordlessly, Asher headed out into the night.

Asher returned to the apartment with minutes to spare. Philippe's frown greeted him. Asher, by contrast, wore the smile of the victorious. Opening his rucksack, he poured the contents upon the table, an assortment of tubes of paint. "At the *Ecole*, there is a window I know about." He withdrew the palette knife. "This opened the latch. The *Ecole* has graciously contributed these paints to the war effort." He reached into the pile and withdrew two tubes, both squeezed nearly empty. "More umber."

Philippe's downcast expression did not change. He turned and looked at the canvas.

Asher saw that the canvas had again been wiped clean. The surface looked the color of spilled coffee. "What have you done?"

Philippe slowly shook his head. "Everything was wrong. The color, the brushwork. It looked not like the Rembrandt but a postcard."

"Philippe, we are not Rembrandt."

"For this, we must be." Philippe swept the old tubes of paint off the table. They clattered against the floor.

Asher bent and began picking up the scattered tubes. "What will you do?"

"We must make the paint as Rembrandt did."

* * * *

Philippe arrived at the Jeu De Paume early the next morning. He unlocked the workshop used by the restorers. Moving quickly, he poured linseed oil into an empty wine demi-bottle. Then, he stole some of the bases for the earth tones, ochre, sienna, and umber, scooping the grains of color into separate envelopes. He stashed all of them in his rucksack in the cloakroom.

"You're here early," the director said.

Philippe felt his heart miss a beat. "When the world is falling apart, I know little to do but stand my post."

The director pursed his lips and stood silent for a moment. "A good French soldier," he said before leaving.

Alone again, Philippe exhaled deeply.

He walked to *Young Girl with a Straw Broom* and lifted the canvas covering. "Forgive me, I may not be able to do this."

Clarice's eyes told him that he must.

Asher had been gone when he returned home, roaming the city without Philippe's papers. He hated it when Asher went off this way. They had both heard the most horrible rumors of what happened to detained Jews. Philippe heard a car driving slowly past their building. He cracked open the blackout curtains and spied the street below. A man with a flashlight walked down the street, the beam sweeping the ground in front of him. Philippe stood frozen at the window, watching until the man disappeared. In the distance, he heard a police whistle. Philippe let the curtain fall back into place. Worrying would save neither Asher nor the painting. Philippe warmed linseed oil on the stove, allowing it to thicken. He ground umber to fine dust, the pestle the recipient of all his nervous energy. Philippe combined the ingredients and stirred until the mix felt smooth and velvety. He repainted the imprimatur, the initial color of the primer. Philippe liked the feel of the homemade paint as he applied it to canvas. He felt in communion with the old masters. His brushstrokes became more confident. Rembrandt spoke to him in his head, urging him forward.

The apartment door swung open. Asher fell inside, doubled over, and breathless.

"What is wrong?" Philippe raced to the door, closing and locking it. Asher had a tear in his pants leg.

Asher held up his hand, silencing him until he could breathe normally.

"You're bleeding," Philippe pointed at a long scratch beneath the ripped garment.

Asher glanced down. "Caught my leg on the fence." His face formed a small smile. "Could have been worse." His eyes strayed to the canvas. He stood and limped to the table, eyes roaming the fresh paint. Asher nodded. "I see the difference."

"Won't you tell me where the hell you've been?"

Asher returned to his rucksack. He laid three envelopes on the table. "You want to paint like Rembrandt. Here is animal hair, freshly clipped from the Vincennes Zoo."

Philippe looked at him uncomprehending.

"We will make brushes with coarse and fine bristles. If the Nazis become suspicious, they will study your painting. Every brush loses hairs." Asher held up an envelope. "Under a microscope, your brushes will look exactly like Rembrandt's."

"You barbered beasts?'

Asher nodded. "A sable and a boar."

Try as they may, the two could not keep their laughter to a whisper.

When they were again calm, Asher again reached into his rucksack. "Here is lead for the white paint." He carefully laid a final envelope on the table. "And stained-glass fragments of red, blue, and gold. Grind it fine and we can make the bits of color you need."

Philippe looked at the small shards of glass sparkling like gems in the candlelight. "Where did you get these?"

"I found them in the rubble of the ruined synagogue."

"You tempt fate traveling that close to the Nazis and their fire."

Asher shrugged. "It seemed right that the synagogue should help us."

* * * *

Philippe seemed never to sleep. During the day, he pilfered linseed oil and minerals for the paints. At night, he mixed and painted impasto, applying thick paint with his palette knife. He drew his brush through the paint to add fine lines and texture. He sharpened the end of one brush and scratched through the girl's head to create the image of hair. Each day he studied a piece of the painting, memorizing every inch beginning with the bottom corner. Each night he sought to exactly recreate what he saw.

Philippe and Asher solved technical problems as they arose. One night, Philippe snuck into the boulangerie and stole a bit of flour. Adding the wheat made his paint more viscous. The smooth, thick layer served to highlight the rough patches he created with the palette knife. Despite his fatigue, when he looked at the work, he felt his spirit soar. *Young Girl with a Straw Broom* began to emerge in his apartment.

Finely ground red glass added to the paint dabbed around her knuckles added the tiniest bit of color. They matched the hands of the child laborer at the Jeu De Paume.

Asher clutched his forearm. Philippe could feel the energy transmitted from Asher's fingertips.

"We are so close, *mon ami*," Asher said.

Philippe nodded. "But we still have the face and the eyes."

Asher steered him away from the easel. He poured each of them a glass of red wine. "You cannot paint the face with fear."

"But I must continue," Philippe said. "The Reichsmarschall returns the day after tomorrow. Already they have moved Clarice and the other paintings to the main exhibit hall for him to inspect."

Asher pressed the glass of wine into his hand. "Rest now, *mon ami*."

Philippe fell heavily into the chair. He dreaded this moment. He had spent hours sketching the face. Squeezing paint from Asher's recovered tubes, he practiced, yet never achieved success. Clarice's eyes, when he painted them, showed no life. He felt his stomach tighten. She cannot die. Not while he still had the power to save her.

"You cannot make art with fear," Asher repeated. "Tomorrow night, you will finish. The oven of the boulangerie will speed the drying process." He paused and looked at the painting. "She will be perfect. All of France will one day know of your efforts. I will pray."

* * * *

Philippe arrived at the Jeu De Paume early the next morning. He wanted a little more time to study the young girl's face. He leaned close, scrutinizing every detail. Then Philippe backed away and examined her from a distance. When he closed his eyes, he remembered every detail. Satisfied that he could do no more, Philippe removed the demi-bottle from his rucksack and walked down to the restorers' room. His key did not fit in the lock.

The director appeared behind him, startling Philippe. "A problem?"

"I wanted to sweep. I cannot get the door to open," Philippe said.

The director nodded. "I ordered the lock changed. Those damn black marketeers will steal anything. Last week, a few supplies. Next week, the art."

"I shall be watchful," Philippe said and stepped away.

The director caught his arm. "Tomorrow the Reichsmarschall arrives. I would like you to stay late. There are always last-minute emergencies catering to that man."

Philippe nodded, his face wore a barely contained scowl.

"May I show you something, Philippe?" Without awaiting an answer, the director led him into the main gallery. He stopped before a large Botticelli nativity scene. "As we will, most assuredly, not be responsible for this masterpiece after tomorrow, I do not mind saying this. Press your fingernail into the paint." He pointed to a thick dab in the corner of the picture.

"You want me to scratch it?"

The director shook his head. "Just use your fingernail, like this." He pushed his thumbnail against the paint.

Philippe did as he had been told.

"What did you notice?" the director asked.

Philippe shook his head. "Nothing."

The director nodded. "Exactly. It takes a decade for oil paint to fully dry on a painting. The easiest test to spot a forgery is this; poke it with your fingernail. If the paint depresses, the artwork is less than ten years old." The director paused. His eyes studied the gallery exhibit. "Some forgers are clever. They use a brick Italian pizza oven to speed the drying process. But even that method cannot make paint completely solid. A bit of alcohol applied to thick paint will make a forgery run. Something about the chemistry."

Philippe kept his face expressionless.

The director's eyes swept over the Botticelli. "I thought an art student might find that interesting."

"Thank you, sir."

"Now if you will excuse me, Philippe. I'd like to spend a little time alone with the paintings."

Philippe went home and told Asher. For the first time since his family had left, Philippe cried.

* * * *

The next evening, the grand exhibit hall of the Jeu De Paume stood in readiness. Everything had been tidied. Rows of easels held art, the finest in western Europe. As befitting his importance, Reichsmarschall Hermann Goering and his entourage had not yet arrived. Only his curator, a thin man wearing a tailored suit and glasses stood by the door holding a clipboard. He talked to the director.

Philippe walked among the paintings with a cloth, wiping at unseen dust. Behind him, another worker did the same. He paused before Clarice and cleaned her frame. With his fingernail, he sought to pry up the tarnished brass title plate.

He felt the plate loosen. Before he could work it free, he was pushed aside. Philippe fell to the floor. The other worker grabbed *Young Girl with a Broom*. He shoved Clarice into a rucksack hanging from his shoulder and ran toward the front. Philippe grabbed at his ankles but missed. Crawling to his knees, he saw the curator's eyes widened. Recognition passed across the German's face. With his back turned, however, the director failed to see the oncoming thief. Like a clumsy dance partner, the director stepped into the curator's path, blocking his way. The thief shouldered past them and disappeared around a corner.

Philippe collected his identity papers, which had fallen from his pocket in the collision, then he raced toward the two men. "I did not hear the doors. I don't think he has left the building."

The curator paused briefly to translate the burst of frantically spoken French.

"There!" Philippe pointed, "he is escaping."

The thief pushed through the outer doors and burst into the night.

Philippe, the director, and the curator all collided with one another in their struggle to pursue the criminal.

Philippe broke free first, followed by the curator.

"Chase him," shouted the director. "I shall alert the gendarme."

Philippe and the curator dashed outside. The thief ran swiftly, weaving through the pedestrian traffic. They pursued the man, running through the Tuileries Garden before cutting to the Rue de Rivoli.

The curator stopped and drew a Luger from beneath his jacket. He aimed his pistol.

Philippe pushed his arm into the air as a shot discharged. "That is the Louvre!" Philippe said, gasping for breath. "You cannot shoot into the Louvre. Think of the art."

A crowd watched them.

"I shall catch him," Philippe said. "I shall do it for Rembrandt."

The thief's lead had lengthened. Philippe ran as a man possessed. The thief looked back. Each glimpse behind him slowed the man. Philippe felt the gap narrowing. Behind him, Philippe could hear the footsteps of the curator pounding upon the pavement. He heard the German gasping for breath.

His quarry neared the bonfire. Philippe saw that only a small crowd had gathered tonight. He would not lose sight of his prey.

The man struggled with his rucksack. Philippe gained more ground. Only a few more meters and he would catch him.

At the outer ring of the bonfire crowd, the man suddenly pulled the painting free. "Let me through," he cried. "I have decadent art."

The guards tending the fire allowed him to pass. He tore the painting free from the frame and cast them both into the flames. Then he disappeared into the darkness existing outside the firelight.

Philippe forgot about him. He saw only the burning painting. The oils and varnish ignited quickly. He snatched at the artwork. The intense heat burned his hands. The guards grabbed him and threw him to the ground.

"Jew lover," they shouted. One guard raised his foot to stomp him.

"Stop," the curator demanded. He held up his hand, displaying his identification. The senior guard leaned forward, studying the papers, then slowly lowered his foot and backed away scowling.

Philippe crawled to his feet. He looked at his blistering fingers. "I am sorry. I tried to save the painting." He showed the curator a charred corner he held.

The curator took the fragment of the Old Master's work. He examined the back and the front of the canvas in the firelight. He pressed it with his fingernail. He brought the charred corner to his nose and smelled it.

Philippe walked to the edge of the fire and stared into the flame. He picked up a stick and worked something to the edge. Wrapping his hand in his shirt, he picked it up and returned to the curator. He showed the man the title plate, *Young Girl with a Straw Broom.* "I am sorry, sir."

The curator flicked the burned corner of the painting into the flame. "That is alright, son. The Reichsmarschall prefers bigger paintings."

Philippe looked to the brass plate. "What shall I do with this?"

The curator dismissed it with a flick of his hand. "Keep it. Perhaps some crazy Frenchman will trade you a vin rouge for it."

* * * *

Philippe walked slowly to the Jeu De Paume. There, he found a clean cotton rag and wrapped his injured hand. Peeking into the exhibit hall, he saw Reichsmarschall Goering studying the art on display. The director stood behind him, his face frozen in a tight smile. The easel that once held the Rembrandt had disappeared. The other stands quickly rearranged to fill the gap. It was as if the painting had never existed. Philippe collected his rucksack from the cloakroom and returned home.

Asher entered the apartment moments before before curfew. He seated himself in front of the fireplace and accepted a glass of wine from Philippe.

"You took a great risk pausing to swap rucksacks," Philippe said.

Asher nodded. "You took a great risk sneaking into work without papers. There is always risk in war."

Philippe pulled the small painting from his bag. He displayed it on the mantle. From there, the young girl's eyes watched the entire room. "But it was so much easier to forge one corner of a masterpiece than an entire painting."

"And linseed oil is very flammable," Asher added.

From his pocket, Philippe withdrew the brass nameplate. He rested it on the frame of *Young Girl with a Straw Broom.* "We shall have to get some old nails to attach it. We don't want the painting to look like a forgery."

✗

Mark Thielman is a criminal magistrate, and former prosecutor. He is the current president of the North Dallas chapter of Sisters in Crime. Mark is the author of more than 40 published short stories. His work has appeared in *Alfred Hitchcock's Mystery Magazine*, *Black Cat Weekly*, and *Mystery Magazine* as well as numerous anthologies. Severn River Publishing will release his first novel, *The Devil's Kitchen*, in April 2025.

THE SAWMILL SALVATION

JACKIE ROSS FLAUM

I shot a man when I was eleven. Considering what went on in Cobb Hollow, Kentucky, back then not much was made of it.

My father owned sawmills in Eastern Kentucky, and the one in Drake County near the hollow didn't make much. By the spring of 1956 thieving there grew intolerable. Even for Daddy. Nobody could see it then, but everything started there.

That spring rogue timbermen cut trees from the backside of land inherited by my father and stole acres of timber. Equipment went missing and newly cut boards disappeared from stacks. Even a light on a tall pole near the office that showed everything in the mill didn't stop the crooks.

"Unless you do something, Henry, people will think they can get away with anything," my mother fussed as she washed the dinner dishes. I dried. Kitchen work was women's work then.

"How do you suggest I stop it? Punch somebody?" Daddy flexed an arm muscle. He loved to claim he was proud of being a tackling dummy on Coach Bear Bryant's Kentucky football team. Truth is, he was a starting tight end.

"Suppose I could sleep in the sawmill trailer for a while," he went on.

Mom rolled her eyes at Daddy and handed me a pot. "Here, Judy. Why doesn't the sheriff get on up there?"

"He should. But we're not talking about something here in Pittsfield," Daddy said. "The mill is way out in the county, in the hills. Drake County Sheriff's not going up Cobb Holler too often."

Cobb Hollow had a reputation for folks settling their differences with rifles, knives, and fists. From the stories I overheard, folks went missing on a regular basis. Especially those who fooled with George Cobb, a bear of a man living at the head of the hollow. To a nine-year-old like me, the whole place looked like nothing but rocks, trees, and weathered shacks overrun with snarling dogs, gap-toothed adults, and sad-faced kids.

"I'll go to Cobb Holler Monday, ask around. Then I'll go talk to Joe Brown about it." Daddy scratched his head of wavy brown hair and winked at me. I had inherited his hair and brown eyes.

Mom harrumphed. "Mill manager can't do much about it without your okay."

"Tomorrow."

"Can I go?" I piped up.

Nothing made me happier than to bounce beside Daddy in the Ford pick-up with questionable springs and wave to people along the country roads. I learned the etiquette of calling out to the house, then not getting out of the truck unless invited. Don't eat anything, even if asked, since most folks needed every bite. Keep anything offered in a sack tightly closed, especially if it moved.

My father knew the Cobb Hollow families from years of collecting rent, owning the mills, and stopping for hot dogs at the only grocery store for miles. He loved eating those dogs with folks. I thought Mom's hot dogs tasted better.

As we drove along the narrow, paved county road, Daddy would wave and say things like, "Those people have more kids than good sense." Or "The man on the porch over yonder won the Medal of Honor." Or "See Mrs. Lawrence, that old woman who owns the meanest dogs in Cobb Holler? She taught math at the University of Kentucky."

Before he went to the mill to see about the thieving, Daddy asked around. We stopped at the Blantons, who owned hay fields next to the grocery, and the Johnsons, who farmed corn next door to them. Then we got to the head of the hollow.

I figured Daddy would ask George Cobb about the thieving. What I wanted to know was if the gossip was true. Did Mr. Cobb really kill someone?

Mr. Cobb's property was two miles from the latest mill site straight up the hollow road. He, his wife, and four children lived on land with a beat-up cabin, an outhouse, a pig pen, one car on cinder blocks, and an old truck parked in the dirt road. A lone cow swished her tail in knee-deep grass.

Daddy stopped the truck, reached into the glove box for a handgun and put it in his lap.

"Stay put. And don't touch this, Judy," he muttered. "But if you do, remember what I taught you."

He sat behind the wheel but opened the driver's door, a slight variation of accepted etiquette. After a while Mr. Cobb came out on the front porch, set his feet so he could stand level on the tilting floor, popped his suspenders, and yelled for Daddy to come on to the house. Daddy got out, left the gun on his seat, walked to the house, and climbed the cinderblock steps onto the porch.

About that time George's oldest son Pete came around the side of the porch. Pete was twelve, tall, blond, skinny as a twig. He walked funny, like everything hurt, and had a black eye. He nodded to my father, then took off, walking fast but stiff like every step pained.

After a while Daddy came back to the truck, hands in his pockets jingling his change against his small cross. When he did that at home my younger brother and I knew somebody was in trouble. His face was candy apple red. He took hold of the gun and climbed into the truck.

"Let's go." Daddy started the truck, keeping the gun in his lap. Once we reached the paved road, he slid it into the glove box again.

Daddy stayed quiet through the whole ride to the mill and paid attention to the road instead of the people alongside it. When we pulled up to the rusted house trailer that served as the mill office and climbed down from the truck, he drew a big breath.

"Well. How about a hello for Mr. Brown, Judy?"

"Hello, sir."

Joe Brown sported a bulbous nose, a souvenir of his prize fighting days. Despite his tobacco-chawing, Mr. Brown rose in my estimation when I learned he boxed.

"Henry, you gotta do somethin'," Mr. Brown said as he courteously spit tobacco juice away from our shoes.

"I've been thinking on it, Joe," my father said. "I'm callin' a meeting with all the men tomorrow, if you can round them up. Then I'm gonna build a guardhouse and hire somebody to watch at night."

"Got a man in mind?" Joe asked.

"Roy Taylor." Roy was a new widower with the reputation of being mean as a snake.

"Yelp, Roy needs to feel he's worth somethin'," Mr. Brown said. "You wanting to start building now?"

Daddy gritted his teeth. "I do."

"Figured," chuckled Mr. Brown.

Daddy and Mr. Brown cut the slats and flooring for the guardhouse right then. For a while I helped hold the boards while the two men nailed the floor together. The guardhouse would stand near the light pole so Daddy could run electricity into the new building for a lamp and heat.

All the measuring and nailing got boring. I wandered off.

Workers, dressed in torn overalls or duck cloth breeches, nodded to me. Young men stacked the boards as they came off the saw line, and the older men operated the machines moving the logs along the line to saws. Their brows were deeply creased. Their jowls sagged. None of them looked like the bank presidents and gas company officers who came to parties at my house.

Sawdust flew out of a chute outside the metal building where the big saws whined. I drew close to the huge pile of sawdust. When two or three piles grew too big, Daddy would pack up the mill and move a few miles closer to where the timber was cut.

This single pile almost reached the top of the sawmill, and the air smelled sweet with the lifeblood of pine, maple, and oak. Why not jump in?

"There's dead bodies under that dust," warned a voice.

I whirled around. "Oh, you're Pete Cobb. How'd you get here so fast?"

"Short-cut. Path 'tween the maple and oak yonder. I know all the short-cuts around the mills. And you're Judy, Mr. Randall's oldest." He had both hands on his knees so he could look me eye to eye—that is, with the one blue eye that wasn't swollen shut. His grin charmed me on the spot.

"Dead bodies, huh?" I challenged.

He straightened up and hooked his thumbs in his jeans' belt loops.

"I heard rattlesnakes build nests in the dust." I could play the one-upman-ship game. "A-and a big sawdust pile can swallow a grown man whole."

Pete laughed real loud. "How you figure them dead bodies get in there?"

He had me. "Ever see a sawdust fire?"

"I did. Come let me show ya." Pete motioned for me to follow. I did, walking around the pile that already spilled into the woods. Spring briars grabbed at my pant hems.

"Are you okay?" I hesitated. "Would it be forward of me to ask?"

"Ain't ever forward to ask how someone's feelin'." He took a breath. "I've been better."

"Sorry." I didn't know what else to say. He must know his father was awful.

"See there, that black place up near the top of that pile?" Pete pointed. "One day it began to smoke. Just a little puff, a tiny cloud. Then it grew. The men had to rake and douse it before the fire got bigger. Good thing somebody caught it in time."

I laughed, a little awed. "It was you. You caught it!"

"Judy! Let's go," Daddy called.

I looked at the sweet-smelling sawdust pile once more.

"I bet flopping on my back and making angel wings in the sawdust would be more fun than jumping in a bunch of fall leaves."

He whispered, "It is!"

I walked around to the mill office giggling.

Daddy mopped his brow. "Get some of the boys and finish, Joe. I'll be out tomorrow."

"Shore will, Henry. Think about Roy Taylor, will ya? He just got out of, uh," Mr. Brown glanced at me. "Roy could shore use a job. Bye, Judy."

"Good-bye, Mr. Brown. I hope to see you tomorrow." I waved.

I don't know what I expected, but late the next afternoon when Daddy and I drove up there was a tiny house. It was crude, raw wood covered with tar paper, and a tin roof to keep out the rain. Inside there was barely enough space for the small table and chair we brought from our basement. The mill's pole light began to click, click, and flicker on as the furniture went into the guardhouse.

Daddy stood in the Ford's bed and put his hands in his pockets. I felt a shiver. Quarters, dimes, and nickels jangled.

"Now I know some of you borrowed tools and boards," Daddy said, and you could've heard God breathe in the lumber yard. "I understand borrowin' from a neighbor—and I want to be a good neighbor. I don't understand keepin' them. I'd like them returned before I have to fire people."

The men murmured and looked at each other.

"I don't care who did it." Daddy talked soft, but his fists clenched and unclenched. "I'm askin' for my tools back in good shape. And I'm asking, politely, not to take any more boards. I sell them at a low price to mill workers, but I'm not gonna put up with stealing."

An older man shouldered his way out of the crowd into a bright oval created by the pole light. He was clean shaven, wore overalls like many of the other men, but his eyes looked like two ships going to the bottom with their last lights flickering. He cradled a shotgun.

"You all know Roy Taylor. He's starting as guard tonight. Thank y'all for your work at the mill." Daddy climbed down from the truck bed and shook Mr. Taylor's hand.

For two years, trouble at the mill settled down. Or I never heard about it. I did hear Mom and Daddy talk about how the man next door to the market, Mr. Blanton, disappeared and left his family in the lurch.

Then one night at dinner Daddy wiped his mouth with a napkin and answered the phone. He listened, then said sadly, "Is that right."

Our mill guard Roy Taylor had gone to meet the Lord.

"Now what?" Mom asked.

Daddy cut a piece off his second pork chop. "Nothing. Let's see what happens. I've got to move the mill again. Looking at a site on the other side of Cobb Holler."

"That mill doesn't make a lot of money, but it surely does take up your time," Mom observed. He and Mom shared one of those looks that made me want to cover my eyes.

Daddy followed the timber source and moved the mill to the other side of the hollow a few weeks later. Took a month, but equipment got set up. The office trailer floor gave way, so Daddy bought another second-hand one for the office.

The guardhouse had to be rebuilt from scratch. This time it didn't have anything in it, not even a stool. Mom said she'd go in the basement again when Daddy hired a new guard.

That winter I missed Cobb Hollow—the men, the gossip, and even the nasty hot dogs. But I did read on the back of the newspaper that the Medal of Honor winner disappeared.

One spring day I came home from school and found Mom rummaging in the basement. I helped her pull out an old bedside lamp, a card table with uneven legs, the last chair from its matched set, and a folded-up mess of something.

"It's a cot." Mom dusted off her hands. "Phew! Gotta air this thing out. Hand me that patchwork quilt from the rag bag over there. Yeah, that one. I'll wash the old thing, and it'll keep Pete warm if it gets cold."

That's how I found out Pete Cobb was sleeping in the guard shack.

When Mr. Brown told my father about it at the mill the next afternoon, I couldn't remember him looking so serious. He wasn't chewing tobacco, and he wasn't grinning. He spoke in a low, hard voice. I couldn't hear all of what he said, but I heard enough.

Pete's no-good father was beating him regularly, so Pete hid out at the mill.

I pretended I was real interested in how the men cut the logs into manageable lengths so I could hear more.

"…books flung around…school papers left." I caught snatches of Mr. Brown's story. It seems like Pete brought his schoolwork when he fled home and finished it under the glow of the mill light pole. Who liked school that much?

Besides, was I the only person who figured if Mr. Brown knew where Pete was sleeping, so did Mr. Cobb?

"Let him stay. He's the new night guard." The coins in Daddy's pocket jingled, then stopped. "Pay him five dollars a week, long as he goes to school."

"School?" Mr. Brown didn't count high school as a big deal. But he nodded and said something like "…another one, Henry?"

Another one?

"Come on, Judy," Daddy said.

We went up the hollow road to Mrs. Lawrence's house directly from the mill and waited a long time while she penned up the dogs. Daddy told me to stay in the truck, which I bucked until Daddy gave me the evil eye. I liked Mrs. Lawrence. She talked to me like I was grown. Her house had red and yellow walls inside, smelled of cinnamon, and she always had homemade cookies. Daddy went up on her porch, they talked awhile, then she waved at me, and we drove home.

That was the end of it. Until summer arrived, so hot and humid it was like hell weeping.

Daddy and I rode out to the mill with all the windows rolled down. I sang the latest Elvis Presley song, "Wear My Ring," with all the words I could remember, and he hummed along off-key. The sun blazed overhead, and the sky was blue. The breeze tossed the hillside flowers like a girl showing off her long hair, and the trees shook their leaves in pride.

I ran off to explore the mill while Daddy and Mr. Brown climbed in the air-conditioned trailer. The mill had already created a big sawdust pile. It was half-way up the back wall housing the big circular saws and the dust flew out the chute in a steady stream.

For a minute I stood at the edge of the pile like a swimmer on the end of a high dive board. Out of the corner of my eye I saw Pete running from a stand of trees toward me.

I turned around and did it, stretching out my arms and falling into the sawdust pile just as I'd always wanted to do. I did a little backstroke motion but didn't get far. I made a sawdust angel. Then the sawdust felt funny, something hard below my back poked me, and dust got into my shirt. I decided the fun was over, especially with Pete standing there looking like he was about to puke. I turned on my side, and someone offered me a hand.

Except the hand wasn't fixed onto anybody living.

It took me a second to figure that out. When I did, I came out of the sawdust pile like someone possessed of the devil.

I screamed and screamed some more. Sawdust got in my mouth, throat, eyes, and nose. Pete pulled me away from the pile.

Both of us were crying and clinging tight to each other by the time a couple of the men ran over and called Daddy. A few more men waded into the sawdust and dragged out the body.

Daddy whisked Pete and me away to the trailer. Both of us had to wash out our eyes right away so we didn't get sawdust scratches on them. We'd cried so many tears there wasn't much point to the eyewash, but Daddy made us anyway.

"W-ho is it?" I sniffled. Daddy had his arms around me, and I held onto Pete's hand. "Who?"

"Mr. Blanton." Pete hiccupped. His lower lip quivered again.

Daddy looked at Pete a long time. Finally, he reached out his free hand and grasped Pete's shoulder.

"You're havin' to grow up fast, Pete," he said. "I'm real sorry. You'd better tell me now, what went on."

Did he think Pete did something wrong? I stirred in Daddy's embrace. He hushed me with one finger.

The air in the trailer felt heavy and still. Pete's snuffle was the loudest sound.

"You saw him, didn't you, Pete?" Daddy said. "Since you're the night guard, you had to see your father bury Mr. Blanton's body in the sawdust."

Pete nodded. The tears running down his cheeks had nothing to do with eyewash.

"You g-gonna f-fire me?"

"Hell no. Nothing's gone missing." Daddy's hand massaged Pete's shoulder. "Why didn't you tell me, son?"

Even I knew the answer.

"He's m-my Pa." Pete blubbered. "He did wrong. B-but I—"

Daddy asked, "You afraid of him?"

I sure was. I could barely see Pete's head move up and down.

A sudden coldness came over me that had nothing to do with air-conditioning. "What about sawdust piles at other mills, Pete? Did he put people in them too?"

Pete's whole body looked paralyzed.

"You know all the shortcuts to the mills, that's what you said." I took Pete's hand, and it was ice. "You even told me once there were dead bodies in them."

Daddy looked at me like I was a wonder, but most of me focused on Pete.

"A-are there more people in the sawdust piles?" Daddy asked.

Pete began to shake all over. "Yes-s."

The trailer door flung open, and the sheriff pulled himself inside. The floor groaned and sagged with his huge weight. "Mr. Randall. What we got here?"

Hours into the longest day of my life, Daddy and I started home. The sun drooped toward the trees in the western hills. I'd talked to the sheriff, then my mother, my grandmother, and even my best friend to tell them I was okay. I was hungry but sick to my stomach. I could only imagine what Pete felt like. Sheriff's deputies had found another body in our last sawmill site, and they were hauling a bulldozer to other mill sites to look for more.

The sheriff said it would be okay if Pete stayed with Mrs. Lawrence until they found his father and figured out where his family was. Turns out she'd been tutoring him and feeding him supper before he came to his night guard job.

When we pulled up to her house, Daddy stopped the truck in front of her wire-and-wood fence. The late afternoon sun carried a lot of heat, so he made sure to pull under a shade tree. He had to angle against the fence but judging from the rut marks he wasn't the first to park there.

After a while, he honked then flashed the headlights. The wide evergreen near Mrs. Lawrence's front porch swayed in the afternoon breeze. Daddy opened the truck door and stepped down. He reached across the seat to the glove box, took out the handgun, and put it on the driver's seat as he had once before.

"Judy, you remember what I told you," Daddy said. "Pete, hunker down out of sight."

For someone as tall as Pete, that was a lot to ask. Then it dawned on me something was wrong.

"Where are her dogs?" I whispered.

Daddy stepped away from the truck and approached the house. Etiquette had flown out the window. He put a hand on the gate, gazed into the yard, and froze.

"Sweet Jesus." He backed away like the gate was on fire.

"Henry, I'm looking for my son." Mr. Cobb walked out from the shadows of the house. I could see him plain through the driver's side door.

"What happened to Mrs. Lawrence's dogs?" Daddy asked. "There's two of 'em laying dead in the front yard."

Mr. Cobb patted the rifle in the crook of his arm. I sucked in a breath. Who was mean enough to shoot somebody's dogs?

Daddy inched closer to the truck. "Mrs. Lawrence okay?"

"Where's my boy?" Mr. Cobb shifted his weapon.

"Put the rifle away, George. I'm not armed," Daddy said.

"That's your bad luck." Mr. Cobb yelled over his shoulder at the house, "Pete! Boy! Come on out here!"

I could almost feel Pete cringe in the back of the truck cab. He whimpered once, soft-like.

From where I sat, I could see Mr. Cobb's face. He didn't act like he could see me, which I guess was thanks to the shade over the truck. I picked the pistol off the seat and released the safety. Using both hands, I steadied the butt like Daddy showed me.

Daddy backed another step from George Cobb and gave me a clearer shot. But he glanced at the truck like he was figuring how far he was from the seat where he had left the gun.

Mr. Cobb raised the rifle and grinned. There was a black hole in his mouth where several teeth should have been and a crazy mad look on his face. I put my finger on the trigger.

"Daddy!" I screamed and fired. Maybe I fired twice. Or three times. Or more. My shots hit Mr. Cobb and barbered the top of Mrs. Lawrence's evergreen.

"Judy, gimme…" After a few empty clicks of the trigger, Pete reached over the seat and twisted the gun out of my grasp.

My father wrenched open the gate and grabbed Mr. Cobb's rifle off the ground. Pete's father bellowed terrible things as he wallowed in the yard. Mrs. Lawrence flung open the door and appeared on the front porch. Her lips parted in horror, then closed firmly.

"Pete! Judy! You two come on in the house," called Mrs. Lawrence in her schoolteacher voice. "And don't you be looking right or left. Look at me the whole way. Yes, indeed, straight into the house. Come on now."

We obeyed, double time. I don't know about Pete, but I didn't want to look at what lay in Mrs. Lawrence's yard. Before her door shut, I'm pretty sure I heard a smack-crack like someone got whacked. I hoped it wasn't Daddy.

Mrs. Lawrence had already called for the sheriff when Mr. Cobb arrived. So, I guess it wasn't long before a bunch of deputies pulled in. Seemed like a year for someone who thought she was going to jail or hell for killing Pete's father.

At last Daddy knocked on the front door. Mrs. Lawrence welcomed him like he was paying a social call.

"Well, come on in, Henry. Judy and Pete have had some iced tea and butter cookies. Would you like some?" Mrs. Lawrence said. "I'll get ice for your knuckles too."

"I-I'd like that, thank you. I'd enjoy some of your sweet, iced tea right about now," Daddy said.

I gazed into my Daddy's face, and the terrible weight of what I'd done slipped away. Maybe I got up from the kitchen table and moved to him. Or maybe he came toward me. But suddenly he grabbed me in his arms, shuddered, and held onto me like I'd been gone a month.

He finally let go, sat down, and drank an iced tea with us, chatting about the mill and Pete's algebra lessons. Mrs. Lawrence gave him ice wrapped in a tea towel, which he kept on his knuckles as they went on about the heat and humidity. Then he asked Mrs. Lawrence to walk me to the truck while he spoke to Pete.

There were a few yellow flags and markers on the ground, a deputy sheriff, and a bunch of neighbors outside. Mrs. Lawrence walked me outside the fence and spoke to folks there. Everybody was too polite to ask what happened in front of a child.

Daddy came out of the house directly. He thanked Mrs. Lawrence for her hospitality, climbed in the truck, and we drove off.

In spite of all the iced tea, my mouth felt dry. I waited until we had pulled onto the road before I asked, "Did I kill Mr. Cobb?"

"Didn't you hear him screaming? You grazed him in the head. Stunned him. He'll need stitches. The sheriff will probably swing by the house tomorrow to talk to you. But you did the right thing," Daddy said. "Whatever else, remember that."

We rode in silence for a while and turned onto the state road. Billions of stars and a bright moon lit our way.

"What's goin' to happen to Pete?"

Daddy heaved a sigh. "Nothing bad. His father will go to jail and never bother him again. He's got a job at the mill. And he's got Mrs. Lawrence."

* * * *

I was a grown woman with adult children when my father died. At his funeral a distinguished, well-dressed man introduced himself as Pete Cobb, although I already recognized him. He hugged me and introduced his wife. Pete was a prosecuting attorney in Chicago with three children he put through college.

"You did nothing wrong, Judy. I don't know if I ever told you," Pete said.

"Never regretted it," I said. "Still, sweet of you to say so."

"I owe everything good in my life to Mr. Randall. So do a lot of Cobb Hollow's ex-cons, thieves, and men with no skills. Your father made sure they earned a decent wage at Randall Mill and could hold their heads up," Pete said.

I smiled at him. I'd long ago realized why the place was known as the sawmill salvation.

✗

Raised in Kentucky, **Jackie Ross Flaum** became a reporter for *The Hartford Courant* in Connecticut before moving to Memphis. Her short stories appear in such anthologies as *Now There Was a Story*, *Low Down Dirty Vote VII & VIII*, and *Modern Magic*. She has a novella, *The Yellow Fever Revenge*, and the civil rights era suspense series, Sterling Brothers Ltd. She is president of Malice in Memphis a Killer Writing Group.

OUT BACK OF JULIO'S

GINA SAKALARIOS-ROGERS

"Bring me two Johnnies, two Jacks, three Russians, two—"

"Wait, wait. Can I write this down?"

Bettino turned to the boy on the other side of the bar. "You need to write this down?"

The boy nodded. "I can't remember all that."

"Why not?" Bettino motioned the boy to follow.

Ned followed along the opposite side of the bar, watching Bettino move, imitating his stride. They went through the door marked "private" in bright, new brass letters.

Bettino kept him standing, lit a cigarette and leaned on his desk. He watched the boy shift from foot to foot. "You know a good whiskey from a cheap one, and just the right amount of water to dilute it to keep a lush paying without getting sloppier."

Ned nodded.

"But you can't remember a list of bottles to stock?"

The boy shook his head. "I could write it down."

Bettino flipped a pen across his neatly ordered desktop. He opened the top drawer of the well-worn wooden desk, slid a revolver out of the way and took out a pocket-sized notepad. He tossed it to the boy. "Keep pen and book in your pocket."

Ned turned the pen over and over in his fingers. The shiny silver coating impressively slick in his fingers. "I can keep this too?"

"Sure, I have a couple more."

"Thanks," Ned said. He sounded grateful. He was a good kid. Fourteen. From a shitty family, but he seemed eager.

"Big party coming in tonight. New ships in port this afternoon. I need that bar stocked up. Glasses kept clean and ready to go. Mariana next door is cooking some of her little Mexican treats to keep the patrons nibbling and drinking. It will be busy, rowdy. People want to celebrate the end of this war."

"Yeah." The boy nodded, "Damned Nazis didn't—"

"Whoa! You're still a boy. No cursing. No drinking. No smoking. No mixing with customers. Got it?"

"Yessir."

"Now, write this down. Two Johnnies, two Jacks, three Russians, four cheap gins and two good ones. You getting this?"

Ned nodded, writing fast.

"It's going to be a busy Tuesday night."

* * * *

Ned proved himself an asset. He kept out of the way, took the ribbing of the patrons well, didn't ask too many questions, and promptly did what he was asked. Bettino was almost moved to give him a little extra something from the tip jar. He counted out a buck in change, then put it back. Too generous, too soon.

"Come on over here, kid," he motioned the boy to join him at a table near the juke.

A couple final swipes of the bar top, a neat folding of the rag and then Ned hot-footed over. Bettino tapped the sticky tabletop with two fingers, and the boy sat. He gave Ned a smile.

"You did good tonight. Better than good, but don't burn yourself out trying so hard. Do what I ask when I ask without giving me any lip like Old Hank does and you'll do fine."

Ned smiled. "I'll do better than fine. Just wait. Old Hank'll be scared for his job soon."

The kid's family was a shitpot of losers, drunks, crooks, and whores. How they produced this shiny bit made little sense to Bettino, and the kid's draw of the cosmic short straw pissed him off.

Ned's granddad's backwoods bar outside the county line was a rickety shack thrown up for the old-timers who thought prohibition secretly still on and didn't want to do their drinking too far from their fishing hole. Ned's oldest uncle, however, had what he called "more refined tastes than the toothless oldsters" his family served, so he came in to throw down on Friday nights.

That uncle thought Ned deserved better.

"Look here," Bettino said, "you still in school?"

"Sure, once summer's over."

"Good. You make your own living, put your knowledge and your money in your own pocket."

Ned nodded.

"For yourself," he handed the boy the buck he'd earned for the night, and the kid shoved it in his pocket, deep in there.

He'd take in a regular salary of five bucks a week for five hours each day. It seemed like a lot to Ned. Bettino, too. He felt good about it though, and Bettino was a big fan of feeling good.

* * * *

The previous afternoon Ned's dapper Uncle Roy had rested himself in a low leather chair at Bettino's desk. The negotiations had been friendly. Roy made a proposal regarding Ned's employment. Bettino counter offered. Roy made a small proviso. Bettino had sent Hal to get some information from Mariana at the restaurant next door.

Hal returned the news Bettino wanted to hear.

Bettino had passed Roy a cigar, nice Cuban roll, and slid a lighter across his desk. He pointed up at the ceiling. "Mariana's got a room she doesn't use. Up over our head here, but it's hers. Access through her kitchen."

"Weird these old places."

Bettino nodded. Lit his own cigar, appreciated the ease of the draw. "Let Ned stay there."

Pungent smoke floated up from their cigars, brushing the ceiling, dissipating. The men thought on the subject of Ned's independence. Of one mind, but not yet completely trusting one another.

Roy took another puff. Tasted the cigar's leathery flavor. Smiled at Bettino. "Just in his best interest, yeah."

Bettino nodded. "Nothing in it for me. Won't work him any extra hours."

More silence. More thinking.

"You like the cigar?" Bettino asked.

"Good tastin' these Cubans."

"From Julio. You know Julio? Used to own Mariana's place. Why it's called Julio's."

"Sure. Disappeared, didn't he?"

"Nah," Bettino shook his head. "He moved away so his sister could leave her situation back home. Have something better for herself. Start over."

"Ned ain't even got started yet."

"That's right," Bettino said. He passed another cigar. "Put it in your pocket. For later." Bettino took another draw. "Julio is here every few months to check on her, check on his business, help her with the books and such."

"Best kind of relation to have, caring and far away."

"Sure is."

Roy gave a "mmhmm" as he drew in more of the cigar's flavor, blew out some rings of smoke. "Know who taught me to do that? Little Ned. My brother had the boy smoking a pipe by the time he was nine." He leaned onto Bettino's desk. "Know who cut that shit off?" He poked his thumb into his chest. "Keep that boy out of trouble. I'll handle the family."

They shook hands across the desk.

"Family won't like it," Roy said. "Cob's most likely to give you trouble."

"I can handle Cob."

"Not too smart, Cob, but he's mean. He'll see this as a betrayal."

They heard Old Hal and Ned laughing out in the bar.

Roy stood up. "Tino's is a good place for the boy. He'll do you right." He paused a moment, tipped the cigar at Bettino. "You've been where he is."

* * * *

Bettino felt good about Ned's work last night and his own good deed, so he tucked into his enchiladas, extra sauce at Julio's next door the following day, and people-watched through the always spotless windows of Julio's.

Sometimes he wanted a taste of home and visited an Italian place a block over. He found the atmosphere at Julio's much more pleasant; Mariana wasn't at the Italian joint.

She sat down across from him with a sweaty glass of sweet tea.

"Why do you sit here in the sun? It's so hot. Much cooler away from the windows," she said.

Bettino shrugged, "Not much sun in the bar. Tiny windows covered with beer signs."

Mariana grimaced.

How were her lips always so red?

They didn't talk much. A comment here or there about someone who passed. He stole looks at her when he could. She smiled when she caught him, every time.

Gus called out from the pass window at the back of the dining room. "Trouble out back with your boy." His gray head was out of the window before he finished speaking. They heard the screened door smack against the wooden frame and Gus's raised voice.

By the time Bettino and Mariana made it out into the small yard behind the building, Ned was tussling with another boy in the reeds along the canal. Gus waved his hands around, trying to grab one of them.

Bettino joined Gus's efforts, and they finally pulled the two boys apart.

Gus had hold of Ned's arm, and Bettino had the soiled collar of Ned's brother curled into his fist. The boy bucked and twisted. A half-rotted suspender snapped, and he lost his grip on the boy.

"How come you get to move out. I'm a whole year older'n you! Ain't fair, Ned," Carl yelled as loud as he could. Spit flew from his lips. Face red, he kicked out in Ned's direction, but Bettino snatched hard at his shirt, pulling the boy down onto his knees.

"You stay down there and be calm," Bettino said.

"Shut up you wop. I ain't got to listen to you." He turned his anger back toward his younger brother. "Ain't fair at all I'm stuck out there in them woods and you get to come into the city and have your own thing. Why're you so special? Why do you need all these dirty people helpin' you out?"

Bettino knew what the boy meant. He shot a look at Gus and motioned for him to go back inside. Mariana took the cue and followed. They didn't make it halfway to the building.

"Oh, you all stay right where you are!"

"Uncle Cob," Ned moved quick, trying to head off the mean uncle rounding the corner of the building. He knocked over one of the bar's trash cans and kicked through the mess.

"You gonna clean that up for him, Ned? Be his do boy? That's what all these brown people are for." Cob had eyes on Gus and Mariana, headed straight for them.

"He's gonna make you come on home now, Ned," Carl pulled himself up from the ground and shoved Bettino.

Bettino knocked the boy down and intercepted Cob, standing between the furious man and Ned.

Cob stood a head shorter, stick thin in his going-to-town pants and stark white Sunday church shirt. He slowed his forward motion a hand's width from Bettino. "What you gonna do? He ain't your boy. You've no right to him."

"Discuss it with Roy."

The small group stood quiet in the tension. Seagulls sounded their laughing calls as they circled and picked over the shrimp shells and fish bones spilling from the toppled cans.

The two brothers squared up at each other. Mariana hung back by the kitchen door and Gus stood a few steps behind Bettino.

Cob took a couple steps back and broke the silence. "Not eatin' today, old man," he said to Gus. "Don't need you watchin' us now either. Go on."

"Get out of here Uncle Cob," Ned said.

"Don't you talk to your elders like that. You losin' your manners already." Carl pushed Ned and their scuffling broke out again.

Gus rushed over to stop them, and Cob pounced. His speed surprised Bettino and he'd landed a kick to Gus's thigh and a rabbit punch to his sternum before Bettino got to him.

He lifted Cob's lanky body off its feet from behind and dropped him onto the ground next to Carl.

"I'm calling the sheriff," Mariana yelled from behind the screen door.

"You just wait now," Cob said. "We're leavin'. Be back though." He pointed at Gus and Bettino in turn. "You count on that."

Ned reached out to his brother, tried to help him to his feet, but Carl shoved his hand away.

"I'm trying to do something to better myself, Carl."

"Shut up!" Carl got right up in Ned's face. "Ma's upset. Can't believe you're gonna up and leave her like that. Keeps yelling at me and everybody else about how we run you off. Her 'sweet boy'! You always been a suck up so she'd love you more'n me from the day you's born! You and Uncle Roy think you're too good for us all. Ma's gonna forget about you soon enough too."

Mariana had rushed from the kitchen and pulled Ned behind her. "You go," she said. She shook with anger, fearful of the boy's rage.

"You got no right you bi—" Bettino grabbed Carl's arm, hard enough to make the boy yelp, and flung him at his uncle.

He followed Cob and Carl's retreat along the canal and around the building, watching them down the small alley between his bar and the port offices next door. "If you come back here, I'll have my pistol or the police after you," he yelled down the alley when Cob turned back for a look.

In the kitchen of Julio's, Mariana fussed over Ned, shooing him up the stairs to his room for fresh clothes. Gus slipped his big chopping knife from the back of his pants and set it on the counter.

"Hope you're going to wash that before you use it again," Bettino said from the screen door.

"Sure thing," Gus said. The men shared an uneasy smile.

"We have customers out there, Gus," Mariana hurried out into the dining room. She called through the pass window, "You get back to the bar, Bettino. Old Hal's probably put a good dent in your gin."

* * * *

Ned worried all night over the ruckus his family had caused. He apologized to Gus and Mariana. He didn't know what to say to Bettino, so he just did his work and left the whole thing alone.

Tino's was full of celebrants again all night. They'd be drinking this war away for weeks, Hal told him. Ned wasn't sure about that. The people last night maybe, but Ned thought this night's folks were just using it as an excuse to drink.

Some of the old-timers from his grandpa's moonshine shack showed up. They propped up at the end of the bar like they did at grandpa's and slurped their liquor through the gaps where they should've had teeth. Ned kept his distance. They weren't bad men, funny old guys, but Ned didn't feel comfortable around them in this new place.

Old Hal and Bettino chased stragglers out after midnight while Ned cleaned tables and wiped down the bar. He tried to work quick, get it done before Bettino finished. Maybe he could scoot up to his room without having to talk at all.

"Hey, kid," Old Hal called him up to the front.

Ned drug his feet, looking down at the dirty floor. He'd need to sweep. That would take time.

"Hey, kid, come on slow poke." When Ned was in range, Hal hooked a stickman's shaky arm around the boy's shoulders. He pointed at the window. "Make you a deal. I'll stay on here tonight and sweep up the place if you get in here early tomorrow and clean these windows. I hate cleaning windows." His breath smelled like stale gin. It always did. Ned pulled out of Old Hal's grasp and put some distance between them for a handshake deal.

"Sure thing!" He shook Hal's hand up and down, up and down.

"Give me my damn hand back. You're going to make me fall right down, kid."

Hal shook his head at Bettino. "You sure he's alright."

"I'm sure you had more to drink than I saw you have," Bettino said. "Get out of here. I'll sweep."

"No, no, you're going to take it out of my pay and I—"

"Go on before I stop feeling generous."

Ned expected Bettino to tell him to sweep the floors, so he headed for the broom.

Bettino stopped him. "You get the trash out and go on to bed. Been a day for you."

Trash duty felt a fitting end to his day. Hal had already hauled bags into the back room, so all Ned needed to do was take them to the cans out back and make sure there weren't any in the bar or bathroom. Hal always missed at least one.

The seagulls were quiet, but there were croakers in the canal. Noisy, bad tasting fish he'd been catching with his pa since he was a little kid. He intended to never see another croaker on his plate. Miss Mariana had cooked him mullet last night, caught right out in the bay shallows beyond the canal. Delicious, meaty fish. She said she would make him shrimp and put them in steamy tortilla shells for him tonight. He'd never tasted shrimp.

Every time he came out the back door the croakers grew louder. He dropped his last bag and rooted around for a big rock, found a chunk of busted concrete from the crumbling slab out the back door.

When he chucked it into the canal, the fish silenced for a moment. It hadn't sounded right though when the chunk hit the canal. No splash, like it hit bottom too soon. He'd put it well into the reeds though. Should've splashed good.

The light from inside shone too dim out the door and the bulb outside was busted. He moved closer to the canal. Gooseflesh rose on his arms. He had that wrong feeling. No reason really, maybe the tide was low. Maybe he'd not thrown the chunk of concrete as far as he thought. The croakers cranked up. A warning noise, that's what it sounded like now.

Ned stopped inches from the soles of a man's shoes, toes down in the muck at the edge of the reeds. The rest of the man hidden. Ned kicked out in panic at one of the feet. It moved but the man didn't. The way it moved looked wrong. He recognized the letters carved into the soles. Uncle Cob always did this to his shoes. No one could steal them that way. Not that anyone would want to. Uncle Cob never had a new pair of shoes his whole life. He found old ones and put new soles on them. Then carved his name in.

Gus and Bettino both heard the boy's screams. They each ran out of their establishments with weapons at the ready. Gus had his chopping knife, and Bettino had the bat that rested inside the backroom door.

There weren't any stars, Bettino noticed. One of those details that always seared into focus during crisis moments. Something to distract the mind maybe. Clouds, he thought, must be some rain coming. He saw Ned moving slowly back from the reeds. Gus got there first, catching him when he fell.

* * * *

They had rolled Cob onto his back and Ned had fainted behind Bettino and Gus again when his lobbed chunk of concrete rolled off of his uncle's back. Mariana carried him inside. Bettino and Gus conferred for the briefest of moments and called Roy. Perhaps they should have called the police, but neither Gus nor Bettino wanted to spend any time under their scrutiny. Someone had stove in Cob's head. No large rocks or chunks of concrete lay conveniently covered in blood near the body, so both men knew the bar and the restaurant would be the first points of search.

Cob didn't look so angry anymore. He looked waterlogged, his red hair a small fan in the water. His brother stared down at him, at the small pinfish darting in for nibbles.

"He looks peaceful like that when he sleeps," Roy said.

Bettino couldn't tell if this was a simple observation or some sort of fond epitaph.

"We should pull him out of the water," Gus said. "Ain't right letting the little fish get at him like that."

They grabbed his heels and pulled Cob all the way out of the water, but not too far. He remained mostly in the battered reeds where he'd fallen.

Roy remained quiet. He looked away from his brother, out into the canal and beyond the small spit of land to the bay beyond. The canal's end in a drainage outlet lay not too far along from where they stood. Bettino imagined he could see the plan forming on Roy's face, and he didn't like it.

Gus saw it too. He didn't want any part of this. He left the two white men and the dead white man. Mariana wouldn't want him involved, he told himself. She liked the Italian fellow, but she liked Gus too, and she'd understand why he couldn't do this. She would understand better than them both why such as he and she couldn't be mixed up anymore in the death of even a worthless man like Cob.

In the end, Roy and Bettino compromised. They tied a rope around Cob's legs and hauled him along the canal and the seawall in the darkest part of the night. No one docked at the small bay marina since last summer's storm tore up most of the slips and piers. Roy tied a half of a cinderblock from outside the marina dry dock around his brother's ankles. Cob slipped out into the bay like he belonged there, weighed down by that chunk of concrete just enough to keep him bobbing along but not fully sinking.

"Someone'll find him far enough from here to keep the cops away," Roy said.

Bettino hoped this would hold true. He put a hand on Roy's shoulder.

"Never got along with him anyway," Roy said. He pulled the cigar Bettino had given him from his inner pocket and lit it up. They didn't stay to watch Cob bob away, no reason to linger.

* * * *

The next morning dawned, and no one talked about the night's events. They all went quietly about their usual routines until Saturday morning, two days later.

Mariana called Bettino at home; she called Gus at home. She wandered up and down the street looking for the boy in the few small alleyways. She worried along the canal, sweeping the handle of her broom through the reeds, remembering the time her cousin had drowned in shallows back home. When Bettino arrived, Mariana was out in the street, talking to a group of sailors more interested in her than her pleas for help.

Bettino shooed them away.

"Go down to the ships, Tino. He's there, running away. He's scared."

Bettino did as Mariana asked. He found the boy staring out at the ships. He could see Ned scanning for openings, choosing the ship he would stow away on. Just like Bettino had as a boy, leaving Italy behind, hoping all the pain of his family would not follow him across the sea.

He told the boy, "No need to run away."

Ned cried quietly. "It's my fault. It wouldna happened if Cob hadn't been coming back for me."

"It's not your crime."

"Somebody'd a done it to him eventually, anyway," Gus said from behind them. He looked grim when Ned and Bettino turned to him. He stood twisting his apron in his hands.

"Something's wrong," Ned said. He knew this sign of worry. Had seen it every day in his grandmother until the day she died in her kitchen, fixing hash for his grandfather.

Gus nodded. "They found that body on down the bay. The bloat floated it right up onto the beach there at the Navy yard."

This was barely a mile away.

"Cops is at your place now," Gus continued. "Someone told them the boy was workin' there with you and they want to talk to him."

Ned was shaking his head, the rest of his body tensing up to follow suit. Bettino pulled him closer, knelt to look into the boy's eyes. "They aren't going to think you could have done this."

"Yeah," Gus said. "You were in the bar all night. Lots of people seen you. You got an alibi."

Bettino walked Ned back to the bar. He dropped a hand on Gus's shoulder and squeezed it firmly. Gus smiled back, still uneasy.

Ned stopped quick when he saw Carl with the cops outside the bar. Bettino stumbled into him and tripped Gus. All three of them went down.

"Now look at that," one of the officers laughed. "We got us Three Stooges here."

Carl laughed along with him, staring at Ned.

"You boys go on," Captain Anderson said, "I need to talk to these men and Roy about the altercation you all had yesterday afternoon."

The boys didn't move for a moment, Ned staring down Carl and Carl evading their Uncle Roy's gaze.

"Go on now," Roy said.

Carl and Ned chose to squelch down the muddy alley back onto the canal. Ned didn't want to go back there, but he couldn't tell Carl why. He couldn't tell Carl anything.

Ned sat on the slab outside the back door of the bar, watching Carl kick around in the reeds. He plunged his hands into the water. "These little fish is fast."

Those little fish have bits of Uncle Cob in them, Ned thought. And there's Carl, Cob's favorite nephew, the one he'd chosen to teach all his ways, the one who hadn't hid behind momma when Cob came stomping in the front door, playing in the muck their uncle died in.

"Get out of there," Ned yelled.

Carl stomped out of the reeds. "You want to know what I did it with?"

The smile on his face didn't look quite like a real smile to Ned. He'd seen fake smiles before, but this one wasn't quite fake, just wrong.

"I don't know what you mean, Carl. Move on back away from me now. I ain't fighting you today."

Carl shook his head, that smile-not-smile still fixed on his face. It scared Ned, that smile. Carl's whole face was scaring Carl.

"Listen," Carl said. He looked over at the door to Mariana's kitchen, held a finger to his lips and crouch-walked over to the door. He put his ear up to it and gave Ned a thumbs up before he hurried back over.

Carl sat down cross-legged on the soggy ground. He leaned in close to Ned, like they had when they were really little, not so many years ago, and shared secrets they'd each heard the family gossiping about. They learned all sorts of stuff about the people that hung out in their grandpa's bar. Some of it they didn't understand, but sharing it made them feel good. Some people had it pretty bad, they always told each other, some people didn't have families looking out for them, so they did all sorts of wrong things with other people's wives and property or just drank too much and did dumb things to hurt themselves.

Carl had that excited look he'd always had when he thought he had a really nasty bit of adult news to share. He whispered, "Want to know why I did it?"

Ned said yes, real quiet, automatically, his mouth moving without his will.

"I did it for you. So you can get established. Then you can get me established too. I did it with the back of pa's old axe head. The one the handle rotted half off last summer and he ain't got fixed yet. He probably forgot he even had it. I used that. Not the sharp end though, that seemed wrong."

Ned was nodding his head. He didn't know why, except maybe because that's what he'd always done when he listened to the gossip Carl had overheard.

Carl had more to say. "Me'n Cob come over here to tell you that you ain't welcome back at home no more. Momma said you abandoned us and she ain't talking to Roy no more either because he helped you. Got no love for anyone, poor little Jenny's gonna be like her. But we're getting out now, you'n me. You's first because you always been smarter. People like you more. But when you get established, you can get me out. Get me established too."

Ned didn't know what Carl meant by established. He knew it didn't sound like a word that anyone would ever use on Carl.

"I don't want to hear no more of this." Ned jumped up from the slab and tried to open the bar door. It was locked.

"Okay. I'm okay. Don't worry. He said all kind of mean things to me last night when we came back down here to grab you, so I was mad anyway. Made it easier."

Now Ned ran. He knew Carl would follow, but he couldn't stay back there on the canal alone with his brother who had stopped acting like a brother years ago, listening to some sort of plan that started with Uncle Cob's murder and made no sense. Had no end.

* * * *

Bettino heard the boy's feet pounding down the cracking concrete sidewalk and side-stepped quick out of the restaurant door to catch him. No need for him to hear the foolishness going on in there.

Ned plowed into Bettino's arms, pushing hard against him to get into the restaurant.

"Whoa, Ned, hold on." Bettino hugged Ned close, holding him until he went still.

The boy whispered something. Real quiet, cracking, all Bettino caught was the other boy's name. He stood there holding Ned, half in the restaurant, the door resting against his back, the pressure encouraging Bettino to move them inside, to end the senselessness happening in there.

"Let me tell, Mr. Bettino, please let me tell. I don't want none of y'all in with the law because of me."

He released Ned and followed the boy into Julio's.

Carl shuffled out of the kitchen at the same time, a crazy grin on his face. He winked at Ned, and the boy lost heart. Bettino saw Ned's shoulders slump, his feet slow, then stop, his head down.

"Now boys," Captain Anderson said. "We may need your help here."

Another officer had Gus's arm in his right hand and Mariana's in his left.

Roy began to protest, yet again, uselessly. Captain Anderson cut him off and held a hand up to Bettino as well. "Now I've heard all you two have to say. Unless you want me to start looking at the two of you as potential suspects, I suggest you stop trying to protect these two here."

He shifted his attention to Ned, moved closer and sat down at a table. Ned sat as well, without being asked. Captain Anderson waved Carl over. He responded reluctantly, choosing to stand in front of the captain.

"We know that there was an altercation here yesterday between your Uncle Cob, God rest him, and these two over here. He came on up to the station, Ned. Carl was with him." Carl nodded at Ned, but the boy didn't see. He kept his eyes on the police captain. "Now Cob told us he came here to rescue you, which we know you didn't need. Bettino here has taken you on. Not strictly legal, but Roy here has vouched for the arrangement and it's just fine. Cob hadn't worked this out with Roy before he came down here yesterday, right?"

"Yeah," Carl said. "We didn't know yet."

"Ned?"

Ned shrugged his shoulders.

"Alright, now, I know this is all upsetting. Cob told us that Gus over there came after him with a knife and that the lady urged him on. He also told us Bettino knocked him down. That happen? They get a little too aggressive in protecting you?"

"They had no reason to kill Cob," Bettino yelled.

"Maybe not, but they sure did toss him out in the water to cover it up."

"Why?" Bettino demanded.

"It makes sense. You backtrack from where he was found at the Navy yard, and you get here on the tides."

Roy snorted.

"Yeah, yeah. I'm no sailor, Roy, don't like being out on the water, but you know what I mean. Jim there explained it better. Now you two stop trying to cover for them. Maybe they found him back there and got scared they'd be accused of killing him, having that tussle with him and all. They should have called us down, but they slipped him into the water thinking he'd sink instead."

Carl said, "I bet Uncle Cob came back here last night to sneak Ned out. They caught him and bashed him in the head."

Gus laughed. "You got yourself a new recruit there, Cap'n. Got about as much sense as you all."

Officer Jim shook Gus best he could with one hand and Gus pulled against him. "You hush now. Don't make things worse for yourself and—"

"Oh, it don't matter what I say—"

"Everyone shut up!" Captain Anderson yelled. "Anyone got anything else to add?"

"No one's got nothing to say about why my Uncle Cob's dead?" Carl cried out, tears on his cheeks. "He was good to me and now he's gone cause of Ned! You going to take up with this spic woman and her—"

Roy lunged toward Carl, slapping him across the face. Bettino grabbed Roy before Captain Anderson got to him.

Ned jumped up when Jim knocked Gus down and Mariana began to scream.

Carl shoved him down.

While the captain helped Jim subdue and put the cuffs to Gus, Roy, and Bettino, the boys whispered furiously into each other's faces. Carl crying, Ned crying, both red faced.

Carl said, "Please, Ned." They heard that clear, then more whispering and Carl stomping his foot at Ned, then pounding it down onto his brother's foot.

Ned said quietly, "Find your own way out."

Bettino turned to Roy and saw that Roy had already known. "What do we do?"

"Only thing we can," he said. "Give him the way out he's earned."

"We're blood," Carl yelled. "You owe me!"

Mariana had moved closer to Ned and at Bettino's nod she sat behind the boy and put her arms around him as he cried.

"Go on and tell them, Ned," Roy said.

Captain Anderson listened, and Jim reluctantly removed the cuffs from the men before Ned finished telling them about Carl's confession. "Damn," the captain said. "Damn."

"This is on you too. You made me do it! You ain't going to let this happen are you, Ned?" Carl squirmed in Roy's grasp.

"Come on now, Carl." Roy hugged the boy to him. "I'll come with you." He looked to Captain Anderson to see if he would be accommodating. The captain nodded and Roy led Carl outside.

"This ain't right, Ned!" Carl yelled all the way out the door. They could all still hear him when the door closed. Ned figured he'd always hear it.

Mariana took Ned up to his room. Gus and Bettino straightened up the toppled chairs and disheveled table linens. They handled the lunch service and closed down in the late afternoon.

Gus walked to the bar and helped Bettino prep for opening and stayed on through closing. Old Hal didn't ask any questions aside from whether the boy was all right. News travels fast and Cob's murder at the hands of his favorite nephew was the talk of the bar, but everyone followed Old Hal's lead and kept their curiosity from Gus and Bettino.

The three men shared a beer at the end of the night. This worried Old Hal, who never got to drink with the boss, but not enough to turn down the drink. Bettino reassured him once again everything would be okay. When the boy came down from his room and through the back door, Old Hal relaxed. The boy looked like he'd had a good long cry. That's a good thing, Hal knew. A good, long cry wiped out a lot of worries and fears and emotional mess.

Old Hal hurried up to the bar, pulling the boy along. He drew a cold beer from the tap into a highball glass and handed it to the boy.

Ned took it and walked slow over to the table. Old Hal sat down, his whiskey refilled, and tipped a nod to Bettino and then to Gus. The boy gave Old Hal a smile.

Old Hal smiled back. The boy'd be fine. Now he was clear of those folk out in the woods, he'd be just fine. Even Old Hal wouldn't go out there for a drink and Old Hal loved his drink. Better the boy learn the pleasures of cold beer here, with Bettino.

Bettino, in Old Hal's estimation, was one of the best men he'd ever met. Foreign or not, he was a damn good man.

✗

Gina Sakalarios-Rogers lives in Pensacola, Florida. Her short fiction has also appeared in *Mysterical-E*, *Toasted Cheese*, *Flash Fiction Online* and forthcoming in *Tangled Web*. Her short story "Pillaged" was nominated for a Pushcart Prize and was voted a notable story by StorySouth Million Writers Award.

A SORTIE FROM THE HAREM

ELIZABETH ZELVIN

"The Venetian Ambassador," Rachel said as they entered the glittering ball-room, "has outdone himself in his desire to impress all Istanbul. I am surprised he has not bisected the ballroom with streets of water."

She and her husband Ümit accepted masks from a bowing page boy.

Relations between Rachel and the Ambassador had been somewhat touchy since the affair of Sofia, the young miniaturist. But they needed each other—the Ambassador to remain in the good graces of Hürrem Hatun, the Sultan's beloved, whom Europeans called Roxelana, and Rachel to acquire handmade Venetian lace for her patrons.

"Welcome to Carnevale, dear lady," the Ambassador purred, "our most beloved festival." He removed a leering mask and shook out the fall of lace at his wrists, a swirl of silken and silver-thread snowflakes.

Every Venetian present was festooned with lace. The new luxury was still forbidden for sale to any but citizens of the Republic. Trust Venice to know how to drive up a market! Rachel knew it rankled that he had been forced to offer her some of the magnificent *merletto*.

The Ambassador turned to greet a new arrival.

"Ah, my good friend the Kizlar Agha. Welcome to my home—to Carnevale—to Venezia! It is an honor! Have you met the lady Rachel Mendoza Gezgin and her husband, Gezgin Effendi?"

The Kizlar Agha, Chief Eunuch of the Sultan's harem, towered above every other figure in the room. The elevated sandals and the emerald silk turban fastened with a pearl the size of a pigeon's egg, a jaunty egret feather arising from its folds, were superfluous, perhaps ironic. His skin was a burnished ebony, his robes of green satin and white velvet embroidered with silver thread.

"My Master, the Sultan of Sultans, holds Gezgin Effendi in great esteem. And Kira Rachel and I are acquainted."

The Kizlar Agha bowed smoothly over Rachel's hand and winked. They were old friends. Thanks to her, the ladies of the harem went draped in *merletto*. Hürrem had paid for it, with a nice commission for Rachel. The Kizlar Agha's own lace was a gift from Rachel.

"Shall we wear our *merletto* to the party?" he had asked. "I should like to make an impression."

"You always do," Rachel said. "Let us be tactful and leave our *merletto* home. Will you not bring an entourage?"

"Oh, my boys don't count," the Kizlar Agha said. "They will dress discreetly and stay out of trouble on pain of my severe displeasure."

Rachel enjoyed the party. She allowed circulating servants to refill her glass with sparkling white wine and accepted delectable morsels of Venetian and Ottoman fare. It was a rare opportunity for her to converse with educated, well-traveled European women—embassy wives and daughters. It was also an unusual chance for an intelligent Jewish woman to enjoy free discourse with Christian men. They treated her with respect once they learned she had known Admiral Columbus well and participated in the settlement of the New World. She even greeted some of Ümit's Ottoman colleagues in this extraordinary setting. As long as she wore her carnival mask, as unrevealing as a Muslim woman's veil, and said very little, her presence was accepted.

"The *hatuns* would love these masks," she murmured to Ümit under cover of the music of an ensemble of shawms, lutes, and viols.

"So do the Ottoman guests this evening," he said.

Behind the carnival masks, a few of the staid councilors and bureaucrats of the Empire were breaking the Muslim prohibition against drinking.

"You had better keep an eye on them," she said. "They must not embarrass the Sultan."

During the evening, Rachel observed the Kizlar Agha's eunuchs flirting with some of the Venetian page boys. The pages were resplendent in doublet and hose of dark red and gold, the colors of the Republic of Venice. A few daring eunuchs flirted with masked European ladies who must be attendants to the Ambassador's lady and other high-born female guests. Ordinarily the slaves of the stifling, perfumed harem never got a night out. And ordinarily, a European lady in Istanbul never met a Palace eunuch. Rachel hoped the apocryphal tales the boys were recounting were not too outrageous. She had heard that Carnevale was a period of license. In Venice, masked revelers took over the city for weeks. Here in Istanbul, it was limited to one great house and a single night. On the other hand, many of the guests were completely unmoored from the world they knew.

Candelabra were lowered, candles snuffed till only a few remained lit.

"Come this way, come onto the balcony. Venice presents fireworks for your pleasure."

The rustling, silken, bejeweled crowd flowed out into the soft Turkish night. Rachel, who loved fireworks, tucked her hand into the crook of Ümit's arm. She could see the Kizlar Agha's white egret feather bobbing above the sea of heads. Colors splashed upon the dark sky. Each explosion boomed in her ears and thumped within her chest. She squeezed Ümit's arm.

"Gunpowder!" Ümit said with disgust. But he squeezed back, indulgent of her delight.

Rachel experienced a rush of love. *At heart*, she thought, *he is still a*

Taino, a man of peace.

Venice spared no expense to entertain the elite of Istanbul. The display lasted an astonishing twenty-five minutes. It was meant to impress the Sultan's advisers, who would report back to their master that the Empire's fondest sometime enemy had gunpowder to spare.

The Mendoza Gezgins lingered on the balcony, hoping for night air and stars, but they were disappointed. The smell of powder without and illumination from within falling on undissipated smoke drove them into the ballroom again. Rachel was looking about, wondering if there were any pastries left, when the Ambassador approached her.

"May I see you privately? I do not know where to turn."

"Certainly, Excellency," she said. "May my husband join us?"

The Ambassador said, "Of course. Gezgin Effendi has a reputation throughout Istanbul as a wise and incorruptible man."

Waving off offers of escort, he led them through long curtains of velvet damask, down a corridor, and into a round room relieved from gloom by lit candelabras. White marble adorned walls and floor. A small central fountain plashed beneath a domed ceiling painted blue and gold. Lying sprawled to one side of the fountain was a slender figure garbed in the dark red and gold of the Ambassador's pages. A rivulet of blood trickled from beneath the boy across the marble floor.

"Stabbed," the Ambassador said.

"Murdered," Rachel breathed.

"Who knows, Excellency?" Ümit asked.

"Only my major-domo, who found him," the Ambassador said. "I prefer to keep the news as close as possible. Scandal must be avoided at all costs. We all balance on a silken thread here in the Sultan's realm."

"Why involve us?" Rachel asked. "Can you not resolve this privately?"

"I wish I could!" The Ambassador's lace flapped disregarded. "But if this tragedy comes from outside my household, not merely scandal, but a diplomatic incident might ensue. It is not only my career at stake. Venice must not be shamed before the Sultan!"

"Why us?" Rachel asked.

"We are outsiders," Ümit said bluntly.

"Let us say," the Ambassador said, "that Lady Rachel is the most clever person I know. You go everywhere, Signora—the Palace, the mosques, the Jewish quarter, embassies and merchants' homes, the Grand Bazaar, your brother's shipyards. You are trusted everywhere. Investigate this death for me, I beg you. Quietly. I will instruct my people, from my own lady wife downward, to answer all your questions."

"Can you identify this boy?" Rachel asked.

"Of course," the Ambassador said. "I know them all. His name was Marco. The others called him San Marco, because he was anything but saint-like—high-spirited and mischievous."

"How did Marco behave this evening?" she asked. "Did you observe anything unusual in his decorum?"

"Not in particular," he said. "They are all young scamps, and they were quite above themselves."

"In what way?" Ümit asked.

"They were making up to those unnatural boys," the Ambassador said. "I did not know the Kizlar Agha would bring them along. If one of them killed poor Marco, it would be a grave embarrassment."

"Indeed," Rachel said, "a diplomatic disaster. Let us hope it does not come to that."

* * * *

"Dear Kira Rachel," the Kizlar Agha said. "Once again, we must solve a mystery without the slightest whisper reaching the Sultan's ears. I fear I underestimated my power to keep my slaves terrorized while exposing them to the temptations of the larger world."

Rachel would have told him fondly that he was an old softie, but she knew he would not take it as a compliment. Besides, it was not precisely true.

"I must put them to the question," he said.

"May I not interview them first, *effendi*?" Rachel said.

"Ah, yes," he said, "you prefer methods gentler than torture."

"I believe they are more likely to speak the truth," she said frankly, "if they are not pissing themselves with fear. *Effendi*, do you truly believe one of your own eunuchs killed the page, Marco?"

"They carried slim daggers for my protection," he said, "but it is hard to believe they would have drawn them for any other purpose. Why would any of them jeopardize their life of luxury in the harem?"

"A good question," Rachel said. "We must ask many such questions, all of which are more easily answered if the person being interviewed is not shrieking with pain."

"Very well. A chamber will be set apart for your interviews. In my own domain, I can promise perfect discretion."

"Of course, *effendi*," Rachel murmured.

"He is shaken," she told Ümit that evening. "The Kizlar Agha *always* has control of the people and events around him."

"Even now, he maintains perfect self-control," Ümit said. "A lesser man with his limitless power might strangle a few hapless eunuchs simply to relieve his feelings."

"The Venetian Ambassador is answerable to others," Rachel said, "and equally rattled. He would rather it be revealed as a household matter than an affair he must report to his masters in Venice."

"Will he allow you free rein to interview his pages?"

"He must," she said, "if he wants answers. But I will speak to our own boys first."

Ümit laughed aloud.

"Our own boys," he said, "are Moshe and Sammy Mendoza Gezgin, who study Torah and the Qur'an with equal enthusiasm and question everything. But who will champion those poor wretches if you do not?"

"I cannot *champion* Marco's murderer," she said, "if it turns out that he is one of them—at least, not unless he had a good reason."

Eight eunuchs had attended the ball at the Venetian Embassy in the Kizlar Agha's train. They were handsome youths, Nubians and Abyssinians, with even features and hairless cheeks, chins, and chests. Their skin tones ranged from a deep chestnut color to mahogany to ebony. Rachel, who had visited the harem several times a week for twenty years, knew all of them.

"If you have done nothing wrong," she said, "you have nothing to fear. I am good at telling truth from lies, so answer plainly all I ask."

No rumor of the death at the Embassy had reached the harem, nor did she reveal it. First, she asked each of them what serving the *hatuns* was like.

"I remember no other life," Yanas said.

"My belly is always full," Serkoi said. "And I need not hunt for my dinner!"

"I wear silk on my body and bathe as often as I wish," Amadi said.

"The work is light," Ousmeni said, "and the young *hatuns* are kind to me."

"Tell me about the evening at the Embassy," Rachel said. "You were well placed to observe all that happened, so what you can tell me has value."

"I had never been outside the Palace," Tapi said, "nor seen so many infidel up close."

"I was most excited to be chosen," Nasri said. "It was a great honor."

"What in particular were you curious about?" she asked.

"I wondered if the infidel would resemble demons," Gyasi said. "When I saw their faces, I believed that indeed they did! Only later did I learn that those fantastic white faces were masks that the infidel wear as good Muslim women wear veils when they go abroad."

"How did you learn that, Gyasi?" Rachel asked.

"One of the infidel told me."

"Tell me more about your informant. What was his name and station?"

"His name was Piero. He was one of the Ambassador's servants."

"Old or young? How was he dressed?"

"He was dressed in red and gold," Gyasi said, "though without jewels or feathers. He was younger than I, though I thought we were the same age when we met. He was a whole man, and a saucy one."

"How do you know that, Gyasi?"

"He was curious about me," the eunuch said. "He put his hand between my legs and asked if anything remained there with which to pleasure a woman or a lad. I said that for the honor of serving our Most Exalted Sultan's ladies, we give all our manly parts."

"What happened then?" she asked.

"He laughed," Gyasi said stiffly, "and I left him. He did not show respect!"

Several of the eunuchs had encountered page boys who were intrigued to meet *castrati* who might tell the secrets of the harem or be skilled in unimaginable pleasures unknown to simple Venezianos. The egregious Piero had tried again with Tapi and Amadi, offending both of them. Nasri, on the other hand, had enjoyed his conversation with the late Marco.

"He did not lay a hand on me," Nasri said. "Marco is a nice boy. I did not know an infidel could be so full of wit and fun. He asked about my condition in a spirit of intellectual curiosity. Well, he was flirting, but I liked it. I explained to him about how we are cut completely for the harem and those who serve the *selamlik* retain a portion of their parts. He said it seems unfair. I told him I am happy with the ladies, and so I am. What a pity he cannot visit. He would make a pleasant friend."

She was obliged to dissuade the Venetian Ambassador from making the captain of his guard a party to her interviews with the page boys.

"I trust my captain with my life," the Ambassador said. "I cannot have the household chattering, with Carnevale over and a Papal envoy coming to visit. All must be in strictest order during Lent. That is—"

"I know what Lent is," Rachel said. "Are you telling me your captain wished to be in charge of this investigation?"

"He is an experienced interrogator," the Ambassador said apologetically. "And forgive me, Signora Rachel, you are a woman."

Rachel, having met Christian interrogators in the form of Inquisitors in her youth, smiled grimly.

"I assume you reminded him of the special circumstances."

"I hope I have not offended you."

"They will talk more freely to a woman and an outsider, Excellency," she said. "My sole desire is to ascertain the truth."

The page boys, of course, knew that their fellow Marco had vanished. They had been cautioned not to speculate on his fate, but nonetheless shared with Rachel several artless theories on where he had gone and what he had done.

"He must be dead. How else would he have left?"

"He loved his place here. To become a major-domo was the sum of his ambition. He would never have gone willingly. Could that terrifying Agha person have kidnapped him and borne him away to be castrated and serve the Great Infidel?"

"He was flirting with one of those boys. Perhaps they ran away together."

"The other consuls have always envied our master his superior page boys. Perhaps one of them took advantage of the confusion of Carnevale to steal Marco away to be his own page."

A curly-haired youth named Nero laughed when Rachel asked if he had been as fascinated with the exotic eunuchs as some of the others had seemed to be.

"Not as you mean," he said. "But I was curious to learn what I could of the Sultan's concubines."

"Did they enlighten you?" Rachel asked.

"I did not believe a word they said!" Nero pouted. "They denied that the ladies go unclothed or that the Sultan entertains a dozen of them at a time in his bed."

"Do you fancy yourself a Sultan as you lie in your solitary bed?" she inquired.

"I am not solitary," Nero said, "except when I choose. One of the ladies in waiting is my mistress, and several others fancy me. Much can happen behind the masks at Carnevale!"

"How many of your fellows," Rachel asked, "are having affairs with the ladies?"

"I am the most popular!" he boasted.

"Nero, I am here to inquire into your companion Marco's fate. Apart from what concerns that matter, I will tell your master nothing."

The laughing eyes grew serious.

"Do you know what happened to Marco, Signora?"

"It is for the Ambassador to tell you if he chooses," she said. "For now, please answer my questions. Which pages are having affairs with ladies, which with boys?"

"Piero, Beppe, and Aldo like boys," he said, "but their *amoreggiamenti* are never serious. Luca and Daniele too, but they care only for each other. Like me, Pico and Mateo are lovers of the ladies. And Marco loves first one, then the other, with this peculiarity—he cares less for the pleasures of the flesh than for the *talk* between lovers. 'Nero,' he said once, 'you must listen to your *innamorata*, not leap upon her like a hungry animal. She is a person with thoughts and needs and knowledge that you might share, if it ever entered your thick head that it had value.' Have you the slightest idea what he meant? For I do not."

None of the Venetian pages, it seemed, was celibate. Aldo, who had enjoyed a brief romance with Marco, supplied the names of three more of Marco's *innamorati*, two members of the guard and an apprentice pastry chef. Any of these might have possessed a slim blade of the kind that had taken the page's life. Pico and Mateo, under Rachel's fierce interrogation, reluctantly yielded the names of the ladies with whom they had enjoyed what the pages called sport. Less unwillingly, they named others whom they believed Marco had beguiled into his bed. Rachel questioned these ladies more gently.

To each, she said, "I am told you were fond of the page Marco. I am concerned about you. If you can tell me anything, if you are distressed or frightened, or if you do not know what to do, I hope that you will tell me. Let me help you."

Signora Palma, whose husband was in the guard, admitted she was pregnant, and probably with Marco's child. She planned to pass the baby off as her husband's.

"I told Marco at the *ballo in maschera*," she said, "that he would be a father. "I *told* him not to concern himself, but he was angry. If he has run away, thank God for it. My husband is a fighting man, and Marco is not. It was sweet to lie with a man who was not scarred and hairy, but I have learned my lesson."

"You must think I should be ashamed," Signorina Alessia said, "but I am not. Marco's station is below mine, but do you think my mother would have packed me off to Istanbul if she had not thought me too ugly to marry off at home? I come from a good family. I hoped that he would marry me."

"Did he ask you?" Rachel said.

Alessia burst into tears.

"How much do you suppose the Ambassador knows," Rachel asked Ümit, "about all these amatory activities in his household?"

Ümit chuckled.

"You can ask him."

"Oh, I have questions for him," she said.

"When I asked you to investigate, dear lady," the Ambassador said, "I did not think you would find it necessary to question *me*."

"Of course not, Excellency," Rachel said, "but we must cast our net as widely as possible to draw in not only all possible suspects, but the true culprit. I have heard that the other embassies may have had some sort of rivalry with yours. I have come to you for the truth of this."

"Pah!" The Ambassador plucked at his sleeves, puffed today with brief cuffs of lace beneath a short silk cape. "Of whom do you speak? The French? The Dutch? The English? Their petty consulates envy and strive to emulate my exquisite and efficient embassy as other states envy and will never equal Venice."

"Yet all the foreign consuls were present at the ball."

"Of course!" he said. "It was the event of the season!"

Rachel thought the Sultan might disagree.

"Would any of them attempt to lure away one of your pages?" she asked.

"Whatever for?"

"To learn your secrets, perhaps," she said.

"Household secrets? *State* secrets?" The Ambassador's face flushed red above his high collar. "For *ducats*? They would not dare. My staff is loyal."

His eyes brightened. "Signora Rachel, if a *Frenchman* or an *Englishman* killed my poor page boy, that would be a most satisfactory outcome to this wretched affair."

"Excellency, I must seek the truth, wherever it lies," Rachel said. "If there is any link between Marco and anyone outside your embassy, I will discover it."

"I chose wisely when I asked for your help," he said.

"Please do not get your hopes up," she said. "The solution may not lie where you wish."

"Speak to my major-domo," he said. "*My* staff members are his responsibility."

"If I may," Rachel said, "I would also like to speak to your housekeeper. The *padrona* and I met, you know, at the time of, ah, the painting of the miniatures."

Rachel's young Venetian protégée had demonstrated her skill, at the Ambassador's command, by painting the *padrona*'s likeness. Rachel had gathered that Padrona Mariana was the Ambassador's mistress whenever his wife remained, as she usually did, in Venice.

"I trust your usual exemplary discretion," he said. "The major-domo will direct the *padrona* to give you any information you may require."

In other words, as long as the Ambassador's wife remained in residence, no irregularities in the hierarchy of the household existed or ever had existed.

Padrona Mariana, at first stiff and wary, relaxed when she realized that Rachel's respect for her authority and intelligence was sincere and that no reference would be made to miniature paintings or to the Ambassador himself.

"I know that Marco is dead," she said bluntly. "Who do you think is called upon when blood must be cleaned away? Does the major-domo or the captain of the guard know that if you wish to leave no trace, you must apply cold water to blood, not hot? Does any *man*? For discretion's sake, I did the task myself."

"What did you think of Marco?" Rachel asked.

"A good enough worker if one kept an eye on him," Padrona Mariana said. "Not serious enough to attract enemies, I would have said, or not deliberately. He was heedless in affairs of the heart."

"May I ask how you know this?"

"By the weeping and sulking of the maids from time to time and flouncing, smirking, and petty rivalries among the page boys and younger guards."

"You see much," Rachel said. "Did he confine his attentions to the lesser members of the household?"

"Not entirely," the *padrona* said. "He held a certain attraction for young ladies married to older husbands. You know how these things are arranged."

"That does not mean that the husbands are always complaisant," Rachel said.

"No," the *padrona* agreed, "not if they find out about it."

"Did he confine his attentions to members of the household?"

"Who else? Do you mean visitors to the Embassy? He would not consort with infidel! I saw him disporting himself with the Kizlar Agha's boys at the ball, but surely he was but satisfying his curiosity. Perhaps he was a tease one time too often. Who knows how such unnatural creatures behave!"

"I was thinking of Europeans," Rachel said. "Perhaps you have some acquaintance among ladies of your own rank at the other embassies."

"There are not many ladies of my own rank." A certain bitterness crept into the *padrona*'s tone. "I am neither a fine lady nor a servant. Each consulate has a housekeeper, whose status is determined by the customs of the nation they serve. None were invited to the ball, though of course the consuls and their attachés were present, along with their wives. I know my Dutch and English counterparts only by sight. But Madame Elise speaks some Italian."

"I would like to meet Madame Elise," Rachel said.

"Would you accept an invitation to drink coffee with me and Madame Elise in my private parlor?" the *padrona* asked. "It would be my honor to invite you."

"And mine to accept."

The French consul's housekeeper professed herself delighted to meet a genuine *kira* to the harem, drink excellent coffee, and gossip about the scandals that made life in a foreign city interesting, since one could not, of course, mingle with the infidel.

"That foolish young Louise de Chalon has been moping since your magnificent masked ball." Madame Elise dipped an almond cake delicately in her coffee. "I suspect her of having been more indiscreet than usual with the page Marco, *celui du corps d'Adonis*. He was always popping in and out of the consulate, and I do not believe it was to see his friends Marcel and Benoit. He was too eager to tell me so each time I clapped eyes on him! But I have not seen him since Mardi Gras. Perhaps he took the occasion to break with her. Charm can become tiresome when there is no intelligence behind it, *n'est-ce pas?*"

"Do tell us more about Mademoiselle de Chalon," Rachel murmured.

"It is Madame de Chalon," Madame Elise said. "René de Chalon is an ambitious young attaché who would have little tolerance for his wife's goings on if he came to know of them."

"Ambitious," Rachel mused. "Would you call M. de Chalon cool and calculating or impulsive?"

"Cool? I should say not! He is very hot-tempered. I happen to know that the consul, who is fond of him, has warned him he must beware of that if he is to gain advancement."

"People are interesting, are they not?" Rachel sipped her coffee. "De Chalon is an aristocratic name. Is the consul's favorite the sort who is genial to all regardless of rank?"

"Not he! Monsieur l'Attaché is proud of his pedigree."

Padrona Mariana leaned forward.

"The most important question about any married man is, Does he love his wife?"

"Madame Elise, I see you hesitate," Rachel said. "It depends on what you mean by love, does it not? Does it count as love if he simply refrains from beating her? Does it prove love if he is jealous and possessive? Or is it love only if the husband wishes only his wife's happiness, however she herself might define it?"

"You set a high standard," Madame Elise said. "M. de Chalon does not beat his wife."

"I suspect that Madame de Chalon is pregnant," Rachel told Ümit, "and that her husband had good reason to believe the child could not be his. Perhaps she broke the news to Marco at the ball, as Signora Palma did, and the husband overheard him rebuffing her. If I am right, perhaps the man can be induced to confess. He was in an impossible position, from his point of view. A page boy was his social inferior. So, he could not challenge him to a duel. Besides, if he exposed his wife to scandal, he would wreck his career. Therefore, he must raise the child as his own."

"Do you believe he planned to kill him?"

"I doubt it," she said. "It appears he was an impulsive man. Perhaps he meant to pay for his silence and was overcome by rage. Even so, with all of European Istanbul present and so many masked, it was a golden opportunity."

"If he had disposed of the body," Ümit said, "it would have been a perfect murder. Perhaps he was interrupted."

Rachel offered her theory to the Venetian Ambassador.

"You may leave it in my hands," the Ambassador said. "I will speak to the French consul. I have no authority over his attaché. But I am satisfied, and he can investigate if he pleases. He will not wish the affair to reach the ears of his King." He shook out his lace. "Thank God Venice is out of it."

"Thank *Allah*," the Kizlar Agha said, "the eunuchs are out of it."

"*Baruch Ha'shem*," Rachel said, "no one can blame it on the Jews."

✗

Elizabeth Zelvin is the author of *Voyage of Strangers* and *Journey of Strangers*, novels about Rachel's youth, and *Rachel in the Harem*, a collection of Mendoza Family Saga short mysteries. She also writes the long-running Bruce Kohler Mysteries. *EQMM* has called Liz "one of the most celebrated short story writers in our genre." Her third poetry book, *The Old Lady Shows Her Mettle*, is currently seeking publication.

WALKING SILENTLY AMONG THE ROCKS

DAVID HAGERTY

The one useful thing Aditsan had learned from Indian school was how to converse with bilagáana. The missionaries taught him their customs and their religion, but more importantly, their language. Often as an adult he'd relied on English to save himself, yet when he tried to compose the words to defend his wife and his home from government agents, they eluded him. How could he protect his family from a dank prison cell, many days ride from his desert home, with nothing but a stubby pencil and a single sheet of paper as weapons?

* * * *

His first day at McNeil Island Corrections Center reminded Aditsan of nothing so much as Indian school.

The new men were stripped of their native clothes and told to shower with lye soap that burned their skin; they were given thin cotton uniforms; their hair was shaved with sheep shears and their scalps were rubbed with powder.

Then a fat guard with tobacco-stained fingers lined them up. "In here, you hobos will live better than you did outside, better than you deserve." He paused to scrape a flake of tobacco from his tongue. "You won't have to starve or sleep in Hoovervilles. You'll get exercise once a day and a bath once a week. You'll even get a job, which is a rare thing these days. So long as you follow the rules."

He began a sermon of restrictions and prohibitions about where the men could go and when, what they could do and why, how they could speak and to whom. There were so many rules, Aditsan questioned how even the guard could recall them all. By the end of it, the prisoner decided to employ the same strategy he did with his missionary teachers: say nothing.

Muted, he followed the guard to a concrete building of stacked boxes with thick wire on one side. Each box measured half the size of his family's hogan. They walked past dozens of them filled with two men in each, then stopped at one where a single man lay on a slab bed with his back turned. When the mesh door clicked open, the man turned and watched as his new roommate stepped through.

Although his skin shaded lighter than Aditsan's, the man was no bilagáana, with black eyes and hair, and a pinched face. He stared through narrow eyes and cracked a half smile, but otherwise stayed still. In stature he looked more like an adolescent than an adult, short and spindly.

Once the cell door had clanged shut and the guard had departed, the man said, "What are you?" His words bore an odd, clipped quality, like his tongue was too thick to form them.

Aditsan did not reply, instead studying the walls, which held drawings of pointy trees and wood beam buildings, delicately rendered in colored pencil. Other pictures showed strange birds with long, slender tails and miniature trains with only one car. Down the side of each ran characters like sticks balanced atop one another.

The man leaned forward and cupped his hands around his mouth. "Hey, you speak English?"

Aditsan hesitated, reluctant to break the vow of silence he'd made, but the man stared so persistently, he nodded.

"So, what are you?"

"Aditsan."

"No, *what* are you? You're no white, no black, no Mexican. So, what are you?"

"I'm Diné."

"Di-nuh," said the man and screwed his face into a smile that closed his eyes. "What's that?"

"Some people call us Navajo."

"I never hear of that either," the man said. "Must be why they put you with me. Nobody wants to bunk with a Chinaman."

Not knowing what to say, Aditsan nodded and moved to his cot, which held a thin straw mattress. The beddings he'd received looked thin and worn—not half so warm as the chief's blanket they'd taken from him, nor the sheep skins he normally slept on—and the springs squeaked as he sat. After going so many years without cutting his hair, his bare scalp felt cold and rough, the bristles as coarse as the blanket.

Seeing this, the other man leaned forward and smiled. "Hey, no worry. This way you look like everybody else."

* * * *

But he didn't. The men segregated themselves, the bilagáana talking with each other, the Zhini and Mexicans the same. Mostly they ignored Aditsan although he was soon dubbed "red blanket" for his habit of wrapping his shoulders, Navajo style, against the cold, a nickname that spread faster than lice. Among the hundreds of inmates, he saw only one other Indian, a Lakota who everyone called Crazy Horse because he refused to wear a shirt or shoes even on the coldest days. Once Aditsan nodded to him when he passed on the yard, but the other man looked away.

Which Aditsan understood. He, too, wanted nothing from the other convicts. He'd met enough bilagáana on and off the reservation to distrust even the most righteous, and these men acted anything but, gossiping about their crimes and their schemes like love-sick little girls.

During meals and yard time, Aditsan sat with his cellie, who everyone called Chang because they could not pronounce his true name. Chang never spoke about crime. Instead, he reminisced about the land of the seven hills, and about his wife and three daughters, who still lived there. "Like Eden," he would say, "but better."

McNeil Island felt nothing like the Eden that Aditsan had read about as a child. Every day, it rained, sometimes without relent. The water pooled and puddled on the dirt yard, soaking the men who took their time outside, and staining their clothes with mud. It dripped through the windows and condensed on the walls, giving everything a dank, cool clamminess. Even the blankets felt damp. To a man raised on the mesas and sandstone of the desert, it felt like banishment.

* * * *

Days they worked on a farm, cultivating produce, just as Aditsan had learned in boarding school, except to him all the foods looked foreign. The prison grew no nuts or berries or beans. From trees sprang fruits with skins that changed from green to red. From the wet earth came gourds in many colors—purple and yellow and green—with thick skins like the squash he knew. Yet when Chang made him taste them, the insides mulched into pulp and seeds.

"That's eggplant and zucchini and pumpkin," Chang said. "You never seen them before? Man, what you eat?"

"Sheep."

"You not going to get any little lambs here. You got to eat what grows."

The prison farm stretched farther than Aditsan could see, and all of it had to be planted by hand in straight rows, as though the order would aid the growth. The work kept the men busy six days a week. As soon as they'd finished weeding one plot, the guards told them to plant or harvest another. For ten straight hours they'd squat and stoop until it hurt to stand upright. Lying in bed at night, Aditsan willed his spine back into alignment, imagining the bones clicking into place one at a time. Sheep herding never felt so tedious or debilitating.

* * * *

A week into his stay, Aditsan received one tablet of paper, three stamped envelopes, and a stubby pencil without an eraser. "Don't waste them," Chang said. "It's all you get." Yet the Chinaman used copious sheets for drawings, as though art was not a waste.

With the first sheet, Aditsan composed a letter to his wife, detailing the prison's strange foods and customs. "Every day I learn how to live here," he wrote. A week later it came back with a red stamp across the envelope: "Write In English." Since his wife had also learned the language of the Americans, he transcribed the note and sent it again, but that left postage for only one more. Could he contact Dibé only twice in a year's stay?

"You buy them," Chang said. "You have somebody to put money on your books?"

When Aditsan shook his head, Chang clucked his tongue like a bird and smiled. "Then you trade." But for what? Aditsan had only the clothes he'd been issued, which he could not give away, and the food, which barely sustained him.

"Look," said Chang and held an envelope containing loose tobacco fibers clumped like unprocessed wool. "I save what others throw away and make new ones." He tore off a strip of paper and demonstrated how he rolled the castings into cigarettes. "Then I trade for what I need."

Aditsan had seen him in the yard collecting discarded butts, yet this scavenging subjected him to mockery. The bilagáana called him "Spare Change Chang" and spat at him. Not even letters from home merited such derision.

"What, you think you live alone, like Crazy Horse? You never survive like that. In here, you got to have partners."

Unwilling to rehash the same argument from his youth, Aditsan looked about him for distraction. On Chang's bed lay a new drawing of a big cat stalking over rocks.

"You know the nashdoitsoh?" Aditsan said.

"What you say?"

Aditsan pointed to the drawing and said, "the cougar."

"That? That's tiger."

"They have them where you live?"

"No. I only see them in pictures."

"Why copy them?"

"For trade."

But to Aditsan, paper was the most valuable commodity.

* * * *

For the next several weeks, Aditsan kept silent, trusting that if he observed long enough, he could glean the answers. His name meant listener, and his skill at hearing the unspoken had saved him many times before. On the yard and in the fields, he attended not to what the men said but what they did. The men who talked tough but refused to fight, the men who claimed wisdom but acted foolish, the men who declared their wealth but squandered everything they acquired. These deceptions taught him how to survive among them.

Meanwhile, he daydreamed of home—of the broad canyons and high mesas, the dry air and stillness—and waited for a reply from Dibé. It arrived as a post card from the Chinle trading post, a black and white photo of several horsemen in Canyon de Chelly.

"BIA agents came last week. They said they would kill all our sheep. They are angry about what you did. I have talked to the tribal council. But they are no help. I wish you were home to defend us."

For the first time, Aditsan cried.

When Chang heard him, he banged on his bunk from below. "No crying, no crying," he said. "You got to be strong here. Be strong." He stood to face Aditsan, snatched the card from his hand, and threw it to the floor. "You get bad news from home, forget it. No use crying. Look at me. I don't know where my family is, and I don't cry. You can't do nothing for them in here."

"I brought this suffering on them. I attacked an American agent. If I had checked my anger, I'd be home to protect them."

"No use to blame yourself. You do what you do."

But Aditsan couldn't. He knew some suffering was due to him—not just for attacking the BIA man but for other times he'd lost his temper, allowed his hózhó to tip out of balance—yet he couldn't have imagined this. The deprivations of prison reinforced the guilt he bore for abandoning his family.

* * * *

With his last envelope, Aditsan wrote to John Collier, head of the Bureau of Indian Affairs, whose policies had precipitated the fight that ended in his imprisonment:

> I am Aditsan, a Diné. You took half my sheep and goats. Then you locked me up for protecting my animals. But your agents are not satisfied. They say they will kill all my herds. How can my family survive when you take everything we have? Please corral your men. If you are a Christian show us mercy. Spare us any more massacres.

Two weeks later, a reply came.

Dear Mr. Aditsan:

> It distressed me to read your correspondence of April 17, 1933. I assure you I have no intention of leaving you destitute. As you may know, our stock reduction program was initiated to protect the lands of the Navajo reservation from overgrazing. The culling of animals is being implemented in proportion with the ability of each family to sustain losses. No one individual will be asked to sacrifice herds in excess of his capacity for self-sufficiency.

I hope you will trust in our good intents and will be persuaded to cooperate with our agents as they strive to strengthen your land and your people.

Sincerely yours,

John Collier,
Commissioner of Indian Affairs

Although he could not decode half the words, Aditsan knew a dismissal when he read it.

* * * *

At night, they heard people across the bay, their music and their laughter carrying on the wind like bird calls. To know such joy lived so close by but be unable to feel it himself made Aditsan wonder if it was part of his punishment, a reminder of what he'd lost.

* * * *

"What's de-por-toin?" Chang said.

"What's what?"

"De-por-toin."

Aditsan heard papers rustling in the bunk below his. Then Chang handed up two pages dense with type. They bore an imprint of an eagle standing on a shield of the US flag. Although he did not understand all the words, Aditsan gleaned their meaning from the title: "Order of Deportation."

"They're sending you home," Aditsan said.

"To San Francisco? But my sentence goes three more years."

"To China. Once your time ends, they're sending you back."

"I got no home in China! I live here. My parents live here. My wife and children live here. How China is my home when I don't know no one there?"

While he ranted, Aditsan continued reading until he reached the final paragraph. "Do you have papers?" he said.

At that, Chang quieted for a moment, then questioned, "Papers?"

"To prove you belong."

"I had. Police took them. Called me 'paper son.' Beside, what good are they? No one hires us. Only Chinese. Only Chinese hire other Chinese, and they don't care about papers…"

Aditsan sighed and let Chang exhaust himself with futile protests.

* * * *

The next day, Chang offered a proposition: if Aditsan would help him to fight the expulsion order, Chang would forge a letter to protect his wife.

"How can you do that?" Aditsan said.

"What, you kidding? It's why I'm here. See these drawings?" Chang pointed to the pencil art that hung from the walls. "I can draw anything. I make it look just like typewriter."

Aditsan studied the strange characters along the sides of the page and wondered how those would translate into English script. "How did those put you here?"

"They say I'm forgery. But I'm not fake. I just copy. Told you, I can copy anything!"

His expression displayed pride at his trade, but Aditsan doubted that two outcasts could fool an army of government agents.

* * * *

They needed an ink pen, but the prison banned them, so they tried to barter. At a trading post, Aditsan could swap for anything he wanted: blankets and jewelry for food and tools. Quickly, he learned that prison operated differently. The bilagáana inmates laughed at offers from him and his cellie. Pens they conserved for tattoos and graffiti. "What's a Redman or a Chinaman need with ink," they said, "when your skin's already stained."

In the yard they found an alternate source. Many times, Aditsan had seen his wife milk a plant for dyes to use in her rugs. By mixing the ash from the cigarettes with water, he produced an ink that was black and liquid, yet they lacked a tool to apply it.

Chang painted with a long brush made from his own hair, which proved too fine for the calligraphy needed to imitate type. "It should be goat or wolf, but where I find that here?" he said. Back home, Aditsan saw potters use a yucca fiber to decorate their clay, so they tried shucking and sucking the plants on the farm until their mouths bled, yet none produced the flaccid quills of the desert.

* * * *

It was always cold. Although radiators clanged and hissed through the night, their vapors never penetrated the cells. Instead, the mist and chill off the bay seeped through the mesh, slipped under the covers, and wrapped the men as they slept. It gave Aditsan insomnia, so at night he would stand by the window, double wrapped in his thin blanket, and gaze at the woods that bounded the prison. Often, he witnessed birds disappear into the forest, and occasionally he saw a fox slinking through the trees. If they could trap such a beast, its fur might do. But how?

The following day, while tending his crops, Aditsan noticed a squash had been nibbled and saw a small hole dug under the fence. As a boy, he'd learned how to set a trap from his roommates at school, but he'd never tried it since. To them, it was a game, not a means of survival.

Using a bent sapling and the sinew of the vegetable, he built a snare and baited it with apple. The next morning, the food was gone, but the noose lay empty. He tried again and reduced the size of the loop. This time, the trap had sprung, but again it lay empty, so he staked the food to the ground with a twig

On his third try, he found the fox hanging, but unharmed. It took two of them to secure its muzzle with a rubber band, then they cut off a chunk of its fur before releasing the indignant creature.

* * * *

Since it proved easier to copy, they wrote Aditsan's letter first. Using Collier's reply, Chang stenciled the heading, then traced the text letter by letter. It took him two days, but the final draft was indistinguishable from typed print.

Dear agents:

It distressed me to read of your repeated harassment of Mr. Aditsan and his wife, Dibé. Our stock reduction program was initiated to protect the lands of the Navajo reservation from overgrazing. The culling of animals is being implemented in proportion with the ability of each family to sustain losses. No one individual should be asked to sacrifice all his herds.

I trust your good intents will strengthen the Navajo land and people.

Sincerely yours,

John Collier,
Commissioner of Indian Affairs

Copying a birth certificate proved more challenging since neither man had ever seen one. They needed a model, but where could they find one in prison?

* * * *

The library opened once a week for an hour, giving Aditsan little time to search. He started at the reference shelf—where he found a dictionary, an atlas, an encyclopedia—but none of them reproduced what he needed. When he asked the inmate librarian, an old, balding bilagáana who claimed to be a professional bank robber, the man laughed. "What's a redman need with that?" he said. "A piece of paper's not going to make you a citizen."

So Aditsan searched the stacks at random. The order made no sense, following neither the title nor the author's name, but rather some random numbering system he couldn't decode, arranged from smallest to largest. Worn textbooks stood adjacent to picture books, *Popular Mechanics*, and religious inspirationals. Not knowing where to look, Aditsan thumbed through each one in order. The volumes smelled of mildew and rotten cheese, with pages so thin that they disintegrated in his hands. In one history text he found a reproduction of the Declaration of Independence while a science book offered a diagram of human reproduction, but none contained a government document. So many cavities gaped on the shelves that Aditsan wondered if all the useful books had been taken. Many men sought new skills in literature—how to defeat a lock or hot-wire a car. Surely, he wasn't the first to need a model for forgery.

With time running short, he grabbed random volumes and fanned their pages too quickly to read. His eyes skipped over murder mysteries and romance novels until they came to one odd entry: *Diary of a Freeman*. The title alone gave him hope, and when he opened the cover, he grinned at the subheading: the tale of a black man born free in Virginia who was kidnapped and enslaved before being rescued. Four pages on, Aditsan saw what he wanted.

* * * *

"Where were you born?" Aditsan asked.

"Chinatown."

They sat opposite each other on their cold cell floor, with Aditsan transcribing, but at this he stopped and stared at Chang.

"Where's that?"

"San Francisco, I told you."

"When?"

"May 4."

"What year?"

"Don't know."

Adistan lay aside his pencil and stared out the cell window at the vast sky, where gray clouds foretold yet more rain. "What about events? You remember the flu in 1918?"

"Of course! How old you think I am? I was already working in my father's grocery—"

"What else?"

For just a moment, Chang sat silent, then his face pinched with recognition.

"Earth-quake."

"What?"

"Earth-quake. Ground shaking and buildings falling down everywhere. My mother made us hide in the bathtub and we—"

"What year?"

"4605."

"It's only 1933."

"Chinese use different calendar. We say it's 4630 now, only—"

Aditsan held up his hand to stop any more diatribes. By counting backward, they agreed Chang was born around 1900, so they chose one year later and moved to other questions.

"Legitimate?"

"What's that?"

"Were your parents married?"

"Of course they married? You think I'm bastard? Chinese bastard who don't belong? Everybody think we're like little rats, running around—"

Aditsan tuned out the rest of his diatribe and hoped that the government would accept a Chinaman's definition of marriage.

* * * *

With both documents completed, they had one wall to climb: how to slip them past the prison censors. If the guards noticed either, they would confiscate, destroy, or use the letters against the men. Unlike most inmates, they received no visitors, so they had no one to carry it out. Though bribing a guard was possible, it required money, which again necessitated outsiders. If they could send both to Aditsan's wife, she could forward them to the right agencies. But how?

For three nights, Aditsan lay in his bunk and stared at the wall, where Chang's drawings showed him another life. He trusted that an answer would come to him if he concentrated hard enough. Finally, he found inspiration in the one showing a big cat.

After slipping his forgery in with the packaging from Commissioner Collier, Aditsan penned a note to his wife:

> Your last letter made me cry. I am shamed that you are punished for my sins. I wish I never attacked the agent who took our animals. But I did. I have written to the head of the BIA asking forgiveness. And he has granted it. Show this note to the agents on Dinétah and they will allow you to keep our herds. The second send to the INS so that our son may become a citizen. And one day, when I return home, I will teach our children to live peacefully with the Americans.

He wrapped both letters in his last remaining envelope and prayed that the language of Christianity, which the teachers in boarding school said would deliver him to the God of the bilagáana, might also save them.

* * * *

That night, as he lay back in his bunk, Aditsan again studied Chang's drawing of the big cat. In the Diné language, the word for mountain lion was nashdoitsoh, which translated to walking silently among the rocks. Finally, Aditsan understood how to hunt without being heard.

⚔

David Hagerty (davidhagerty.net) has published more than fifty short stories, including several others about Aditsan in *Alfred Hitchcock's Mystery Magazine*. He also wrote the Duncan Cochrane series, about crime and dirty politics in his hometown of Chicago.

THE LAW IN AGUATURBIA

JIM DOHERTY

Gus Hachette paused as he stepped out the door of the Town Marshal's office and looked around. At twenty-three, he'd been appointed the police chief, indeed the entire police department, of Aguaturbia, a Texas town of roughly three thousand souls, located in Grimes County at the confluence of the Brazos and Aguaturbia Rivers. It didn't look too different than it probably did in the 1870s. Dirt roads. Wooden sidewalks. But motor-cars were seen with more frequency, and three different railroads used the depot on Railroad Street in the center of town. Phone wires connected the townspeople to each other and to the rest of the world. Small it may have been, but it was fifteen times larger than Anderson, the county seat.

Though Hachette had an excellent law-enforcement record, having spent two years in the Texas Rangers, he and Aguaturbia were, in some respects, not a good fit.

Aguaturbia was East Texas, and, culturally, East Texas was more southern than western. Cotton, not cattle, was king. Plantations, not ranches, were the main agricultural producers. Hachette, six foot three inches tall, with his wide-brimmed Stetson, his riding boots, his prominently displayed western-style gun belt, and his comparatively egalitarian views, was an oddity.

The town had more than its share of troublemakers. A substantial portion of Aguaturbia was colored, and they were "kept in their place" by a group called the "White Man's Union." A lynching some months back, in which Hachette's predecessor had been permanently crippled, had created the job opening, and had left the colored population restive and fearful.

And rumor had it that the Union had affiliated with the revived Ku Klux Klan. Recently reorganized in Georgia in the wake of the success of Thomas Dickson's novel, *The Clansman*, it was spreading throughout the rest of the South. D.W. Griffith was said to be interested in adapting the book into a moving picture, which would undoubtedly cause the revived KKK to grow even faster. Of course, because the Klan was a secret organization, no one in the White Man's Union was acknowledging the affiliation.

Hachette had his work cut out for him, but, with the confidence of youth, he looked forward to the challenge.

Across the street, Henry W. Tanner, a man in late middle-age, with a beard that extended to his chest, stepped out of the bar. Seeing Hachette, he decided to let the baby-faced policeman know who ran things in Aguaturbia by screaming a loud rebel yell.

Hachette slowly crossed the street, as Tanner continued yelling.

"I'm Gus Hachette, the new town marshal," he said, once he was a few feet from Tanner. "You're disturbing the peace. Stop now, unless you want to go to jail."

Tanner responded with another yell. Hachette grabbed him by his beard and threw him onto the street. Then, grabbing Tanner by his shirt collar and belt, he marched him over to the marshal's office.

"I told you what would happen," Hachette said, "but you had to test me."

* * * *

A chastened Tanner paid a fine in court the next morning and was released. That afternoon, Hachette was visited by a man who introduced himself as Bowers.

"I'm what you might call the spokesman for our White Man's Union here in Grimes County," he said.

"Would that make you the Exalted Cyclops?" asked Hachette.

"I see you're familiar with Klan terms. Of course, I can't confirm any affiliation between the Klan and our White Man's Union."

"What's your business with me, Mr. Bowers?"

"I just wanted to warn you, in a friendly way, that we don't allow our kind to be arrested. I understand you had a point to make with Mr. Tanner, but from now on, you should confine your efforts to darkies, white trash, and outsiders."

Reaching into a pocket of his jacket, he withdrew a sheet of paper, and said, "I've taken the liberty of making a list of men who are outside of your authority."

"Well, I certainly thank you, Mr. Bowers. Appreciate your taking the time."

"Not at all, Marshal. My decided pleasure."

* * * *

That night, Isaac N. Flewns, whose name was near the top of Bowers's list, got roaring drunk at the bar across from Hachette's office, pulled a pistol from his pocket and began shooting the place up. Hachette arrived in less than a minute, easily disarmed Flewns, and marched him off to jail.

"I understand you don't allow your kind get arrested," he said to the hostile crowd as he force-marched Flewns out of the establishment. "Easiest way to avoid that is not break the law."

Fifteen minutes later, Mrs. Flewns arrived at the marshal's office.

Pulling a wad of bills out of her purse, she asked, "How much will you take to let my husband out?"

"Ma'am, your money don't talk 'til tomorrow when the judge opens court. He has to stay in jail tonight."

"But he's *white*!"

"That's what's wrong with this damned town. *White*! I'm a white man, but I'm doing my job. Your husband stays locked up. Money don't buy me! I'm already bought, to take this here position of Marshal."

* * * *

For the next few weeks things stayed quiet, but there was a sense that emotions were simmering over a hot fire and could boil over any minute.

Some seven weeks after Hachette had been sworn in and assumed his duties, four white boys ganged up on a single colored boy, ten-year-old Micah Cook, threw him to the ground, kicked him, and beat him with their fists. When they relented and stepped back, their leader, Nicky Crowe, kneeled next to Micah and hit him over the head with a rock. Micah's father, Joshua, arrived, forcibly pulled Nicky off of his son, stood Micah up, and slowly walked him toward the pharmacy to have his cuts and bruises seen to.

Nicky ran to his father, Zeb, another White Man's Union member, and reported that, "Some n— just pushed me for no reason."

Zeb Crowe picked up a sixteen-inch-long two-by-four from the ground, intercepted Joshua and his son as they approached the pharmacy, and beat Joshua over the head with the board. Sustaining three blows, but still standing, Joshua reached into his back pocket, drew a folded knife, opened it, and stabbed Crowe three times.

At this point, Hachette came running up to the scene, pistol drawn and said, "Crowe, you drop that two-by-four, and Josh, you drop that knife."

Both belligerents dropped their weapons.

"Josh, you come on over here. We're going to take a walk over the marshal's office."

"Is I under arrest, Mist' Hachette?"

"No. I saw what happened. You acted in self-defense. But stabbing a white man's not going to win you any popularity contests. I'm putting you in protective custody."

"Gots to see to my boy, Mist' Hachette."

Hachette looked around and saw an older colored women on the sidewalk watching the goings-on.

"You know that woman, Josh?"

"That be Miz Ruby Gillian. Knowed her since I was a boy."

"Miz Ruby," said Hachette in a loud voice.

"Yessuh," she said, obviously surprised to be addressed by name.

"Can you get Josh's boy over to the pharmacy? Once he's patched up, bring him over to the marshal's office. Bring his mother and sister, too."

"Yessuh," she replied, going over to Micah, and walking him the rest of the way to the pharmacy.

* * * *

Several hours later, Joshua Cook and his family were safely, at least so they hoped, settled in holding cells on one of the upper floors of the Grimes County Courthouse in the tiny village of Anderson.

The sheriff wasn't any too happy about putting them there.

"What's that buck under arrest for?" he demanded.

"He isn't," answered Hachette. "He's in protective custody."

"Protective custody for what?"

"He stabbed someone who's a higher-up in the White Man's Union."

"Then why isn't he under arrest? For that matter, why's he still alive? Stabbing a white man should've been his last act on Earth."

"That white man tried to kill him. Cook acted in self-defense. Law says if a man's trying to kill you, you can use deadly force to protect yourself. Doesn't say anything about exceptions if the attacker's white and the victim's colored."

"Well...yeah," admitted the sheriff. "But it's understood. Especially in this county."

"In the part of the county where *I'm* in charge, we go by the *law*. Not by unofficial 'understandings.' Cook's son was set upon by a bunch of bullies, and Cook put a stop to it. When the father of one of the bullies clobbered Cook three times with a hunk of wood, Cook defended himself with the only weapon he had, a little bitty pocketknife. He was within his rights, and I mean to uphold those rights."

The sheriff regarded Hachette in the pause that followed.

"You stood down some lynch mobs when you were a Ranger, didn't you?" asked the sheriff.

"Few times."

"Well, do you think we might have to tonight?"

"Could be. And it might be more colorful than any we've seen in our careers."

"How's that?"

"Rumor is the White Man's Union has affiliated with that new Klan group in Georgia. We might be facing a mob dressed in their bedsheets, flour sacks over their heads with holes cut out for the eyes, burning crosses, things like that."

"Hell," the sheriff said quietly. "Don't know why I let 'em talk me into running for this damned job."

* * * *

When the mob came, it turned out to be no more than a dozen men demanding that Cook be turned over to them. They were all, as Hachette predicted, dressed in makeshift Klan outfits, not nearly as well-tailored as those Griffith would use in *The Birth of a Nation* some years hence. Just bedsheets and flour sacks, also as Hachette predicted. They all held revolvers.

Hachette and the sheriff stepped out of the courthouse. The sheriff, his handgun drawn, but pointed down, took a position in front of the door to block it. Hachette, armed with a '94 Winchester 30-30 lever-action, stepped forward to the top of the stairway leading down to the ground level.

"We want him!" said one of the lynchers. Despite the mask, Hachette recognized the voice of Crowe.

"Why's that?" asked Hachette. "You can't have been hurt that bad, if you're here a few hours after he stabbed you. And if you didn't like getting stabbed, you shouldn't've tried to beat him to death with a hardwood board."

Crowe, silenced at first at having been recognized, paused for a few seconds before saying, "We'll come up and get him if you don't let us have him."

Hachette levered a round into the firing chamber of the rifle, then loaded an extra round into the magazine.

"Any one of you puts one foot on that bottom step, and I'll kill ten of you with this here 30-30. The two that are still alive, I'll take care of with my Colt. Anybody I don't get, the sheriff will. Just put a foot on that step if you don't believe me."

The twelve Klansmen decided not to test Hachette, having heard of his reputation for standing down lynch mobs. They put away their guns and walked off.

* * * *

The next morning, Crowe, who'd arrived in court before it convened, filed a complaint against Cook. Hachette appeared beside Cook in court, testified to what had happened, and asked the judge to dismiss the complaint. Stuck between the letter of the law, and the testimony of a respected peace officer, the judge reluctantly did so.

Crowe, no longer wearing the Klan costume, jumped up and protested vehemently.

"That reminds me, Judge," said Hachette. "I was going to swear out a warrant on Mr. Crowe for attempted murder. Long as we're both here, why don't you go ahead and issue it? I'll serve it immediately, and Crowe can have his initial appearance right now."

Again, reluctantly, the judge acquiesced to Hachette's request. Hachette went into the gallery, grabbed hold of Crowe's collar and marched him up to the Judge's bench. The judge eventually persuaded Crowe to plead guilty to misdemeanor assault and pay a fine of fifty dollars. As lenient as the punishment was, given that Crowe really did intend to kill Joshua Cook, it was the first time in anyone's memory that a white man in Grimes County had been convicted of a crime against a colored man.

* * * *

"Won't be safe for you back in Aguaturbia, Josh," said Hachette. "You told me you've done some blacksmithing. I've arranged for my father to take you on as an assistant at his shop in Wilson County. He'll let you and your family stay in the back room of the shop 'til you get a place of your own. Here's train tickets, and some money to tide you over. Pay me back when you can."

"Why you doin' all this, Mist' Hachette?" asked Cook.

"A few reasons. Some years back, a colored man saved my life. Details don't matter. Even if that hadn't've happened, though, I took an oath to uphold the law. That oath *means* something. Law's got to work for everyone, if it's going to work for anyone."

With that, he put out his hand and shook Cook's. "Notify me when you get there, Josh so I know you arrived safe. And take care of that family of yours."

"I'm sure obliged, Mist' Hachette," said Cook, gripping the marshal's hand.

"Not at all," said Hachette. "Like I said, I'm still working off a debt to an old colored field hand who saved my life."

* * * *

For the next few weeks, Aguaturbia was quiet as Hachette patrolled the town on foot and horseback. But there was still that sense, once again, of emotions about to boil over. Hachette had added a cross-draw holster to his gun belt, worn off his left hip, in which he carried a second Colt .45 revolver, in case he suddenly had to deal with multiple adversaries. His regular .45 remained in its front-draw holster at his right.

One afternoon, as he was patrolling the main street on foot, he stopped to talk to his boss, Mayor Kirk Charles. A group of White Man's Union members were gathered outside of the bar across from the marshal's office. Zeb Crowe, wearing a waist-length leather jacket, was standing at the forefront of the crowd.

"Any man," Crowe called out, "needs *two* guns to patrol a bitty little town like Aguaturbia must be a coward!"

Hachette unbuckled his gun belt, handed it to Charles, and, clasping his hands behind him, slowly walked over to Crowe. He stopped when there was roughly six feet between them.

"Fella insults me like that," said Hachette, "he'd better be able to back it up. Can you back it up, Crowe?"

"You stupid, prideful cowboy!" said Crowe, laughing. "I knew if I taunted you, you'd disarm yourself."

With that, he reached under his jacket for a pistol he had hidden in a shoulder holster and started to draw it.

As Crowe's gun cleared the holster, Hachette pulled a small Colt '03 hammerless .32 semi-automatic pistol from where he'd been concealing it inside his waistband at the small of his back, brought it to bear, and cranked off six shots (the .32 round being a relatively anemic load compared to the .45 rounds he generally used). Crowe fell to the ground, dead.

"Fine lawman I'd be," said Hachette to the corpse, "if I couldn't spot the bulge of a shoulder holster under a tight jacket like that."

A long-time cop, **Jim Doherty** has served law enforcement at the federal, state, and local levels, policing everything from college campuses to military bases, from rural dirt roads to inner city streets. His article, "Blood for Oil," won a Spur. His novel, *An Obscure Grave*, was a Dagger finalist. This story was inspired by an incident from the life of legendary lawman Frank Hamer, who fought white supremacists as the police chief of a small East Texas town.

THE HOUND HEADS TO HOLLYWOOD

MICHELE BAZAN REED

"La Grande Station. La Grande Station. Los Angele-e-e-e-s!" The conductor's chant cut through my foggy brain, lulled into sleep by the rhythm of the train. I raised the shade to see bright sunlight glinting off the green dome and red bricks of the Moorish style palace of transportation that dominated the corner of Second Street and Santa Fe Avenue.

The grand dome topping the central part of the sprawling complex, and the turreted towers at either end made me wonder if I had in fact landed in California or been transported to a castle in Spain.

To a humble PI from the snowy streets of Syracuse, this seemed like the set of a grand Hollywood picture show, complete with extras. No one prepared me for crowds that thronged the station, come to gawk at the tourists from the Midwest and East, who did their own gawking at the palm trees lining the streets under cloudless blue skies.

I felt lucky to see the famous station. The city fathers voted last year to build a new station combining all the rail lines that served this one and Central Station, and work was already underway.

I'd taken the 20th Century Limited to Chicago, then the Santa Fe Railroad's California Limited down to LA. The journey took four days, but thanks to my new clients, the king and queen of the silver screen, I rode in luxury. Mary Pickford and Douglas Fairbanks spared no expense and yours truly, Harry Jerome, PI, aka The Hound, best tracker in four Eastern states, enjoyed all dining car privileges. A fully stocked bar was hidden in my private Pullman car, Prohibition be damned.

Alighting at La Grande Station, I saw the famed Yellow Car railroad carriages shining in the sun, but nary a cab to take me to Pickfair, the couple's mansion in some new-fangled out-of-the-way place, called what? I checked the telegram in my hand. Oh yeah, Beverly Hills. I was about to give up hope of finding a ride, when I heard a voice call my name.

"Mr. Jerome, follow me," said a dapper gent who appeared at my shoulder, kitted out in the livery of a chauffeur. As we approached a huge silver car, I couldn't help but give an appreciative whistle.

"Beauty, isn't she?" said my chauffeur, who introduced himself as Leo.

"I'll say," I agreed, running my fingers along the fender of the 1924 Pierce Arrow.

"Series 33, top of the line," Leo assured me. We set out on the road to San Ysidro Canyon.

I was surprised by how far out in the country the mansion was, and I told Leo so.

"It used to be a hunting lodge, before Mr. Fairbanks bought it as a wedding gift for Miss Pickford back in '19," he said. "Wait'll you take a gander at that house! It's the bee's knees! It's got twenty-five rooms, even a billiard room and an in-ground swimming pool." He proudly told me the pool was a first for Los Angeles. "You mean you didn't see the picture of them paddling a canoe in it? It was in all the papers." Leo shook his head in amazement.

I had to shake my head, too, as we pulled up in front of Pickfair. The couple was constantly renovating it, and I could see workmen scurrying around, but the overall effect was breathtaking. A huge wrought iron gate barred the way, giving access to the mock-Tudor mansion. I jumped out to open it, so Leo could drive through.

We passed right by the magnificent front entrance, though, and headed around the stables and tennis courts toward the back of the home. "Sorry about this, Mr. Jerome," Leo said. "But it's orders, direct from Miss P. It appears your visit is on the Q-T, so mum's the word." He turned and gave me a little wink.

"No problem, Leo," I said. "My work is always confidential. I know a thing or two about discretion."

Leo led me through what seemed like a dozen rooms, each more fantastic than the last. There was even a replica Wild West saloon, compete with swinging door and mahogany bar.

I'd read that the couple was collecting masterpieces of art from Europe, but I was surprised to see Chinese porcelains and sculptures by Frederic Remington. I tried not to gawk, but it was hard not to be awed by the palace of Hollywood's own royalty.

Finally, Leo ushered me into a small sitting room, furnished with a velvet davenport and two wing chairs in the same material. A small side table had a tray full of finger sandwiches, and a fully stocked bar cart sat next to it. Apparently, Prohibition wasn't a concern in the Hollywood hills.

"Make yourself at home, Mr. Jerome," Leo said. "Miss P will be with you shortly. She thought you might want a little snack after your train trip."

I thanked Leo and eyed the spread. I'd feasted like a king in the dining car cross country, but it seemed like The Hound was going to eat well in Hollywood, too. I always liked a little ham and rye, so I helped myself to a sandwich of one and a generous glass of the other, when the door swung inward and my mouth dropped open.

There was the queen of the movie industry, America's Sweetheart herself. Her signature curls shone in the light coming through the floor-to-ceiling windows and she was dressed in a lavender silk dress that looked like something out of a Paris fashion magazine. Which, undoubtedly, it was. I remembered that she and Mr. Fairbanks had honeymooned on a trip around the world, and he was reputed to have lavished her with gifts along the way.

I'm rarely at a loss for words, but as she advanced, her hand outstretched and that famous smile lighting up her face, I could only stammer, "P-pleased to meet you, Miss Pickford."

"No, Mr. Jerome, you must call me Mary, and I shall call you Harry." Her voice dropped to a whisper. "I've told everyone, but Leo, of course, that you're an old friend from back East, come to look for work in Hollywood. Well, you'll find it here!" She giggled at her own joke, and I couldn't help but join in.

Her giddy mood vanished as quickly as it appeared, leading me to wonder whether she was acting now, or then. "Mr. Jerome…Harry…we brought you out because we needed a discreet person to conduct a very, mmm, quiet inquiry. Mr. Coogan vouched for you. Said you helped with a little incident?"

Well, there was one mystery solved. When the telegram from Hollywood arrived, even I had wondered how a famous star like Mary Pickford would know about a relatively unknown gumshoe from a backwater burg like Syracuse.

But back in '24, Jackie Coogan visited Syracuse to raise money for orphans in the Near East. Jackie and his father stayed at the new Hotel Syracuse—the first to sign the guest book, in fact. And as usual when someone famous attracts a lot of attention, that also attracted trouble. When said trouble needed solving, the hotel called me, and I guess you might say I saved the day. It was all very hush-hush. You won't read about it in any of the papers. No one wanted any bad publicity.

Now that she mentioned his name, I recalled that Jackie played in a movie with Charlie Chaplin, and Charlie's good friends with Miss Pickford and Mr. Fairbanks. They founded United Artists together with some other actors and I guess that's how Jackie's dad got to know them all.

"Right, Mr. Jerome?" Mary was looking at me with a quizzical smile on her face.

"Yes, ma'am," I said, realizing as I did, that I sounded every bit the country bumpkin, but I couldn't help myself. At least I wasn't totally tongue-tied. "And I intend to provide you with the same level of professionalism and discretion," I added, hoping to redeem my image a little.

She looked around then, and satisfied that no one was anywhere near, she continued.

"As you know, Mr. Fairbanks and I entertain some high-profile guests here at Pickfair."

I nodded. I'd read some of the guest lists for their grand parties in *Pho-*

toplay during my train trip: Chaplin himself, Thomas Edison, Lillian Gish, F. Scott Fitzgerald.

"We have some special guests at the moment. Members of a certain royal family are here for the summer. We met them on our honeymoon, and we became friends. I'm sure you'll appreciate the fact that I can't tell you who."

I recalled reading in *Photoplay* that Pickfair had hosted plenty of royals. The King and Queen of Siam, Crown Prince of Japan, Lord and Lady Mountbatten, and others. I glanced over at photos on the marble mantlepiece of Miss Pickford and Mr. Fairbanks with folks in fancy garb outside European palaces and Asian temples.

"My guests are due to leave for their own country at the end of the month, but there's been a problem!" She leaned so close to me I caught a whiff of Shalimar as a single curl swung down and brushed the back of my hand. "One of my guest's bracelets has gone missing. It's set with diamonds and a huge ruby. What a catastrophe!"

"It must be worth a fortune," I said, trying to fathom why the royal lady would be wearing it on what seemed like a casual visit.

"Of course, it is valuable, but more importantly, it's officially part of the crown jewels. It would be a huge scandal in their home country if it went missing." She shuddered a little and looked down at her hands, clasped tightly in her lap. "It would be a scandal for us, too, especially if one of our guests—or even worse, one of our own staff—was found to have taken the jewelry."

I exhaled as I took in the magnitude of the problem. I'd expected some minor Hollywood scandal, like the gossip sheets are full of. Maybe someone having an affair with someone else's spouse. Or the plot for an upcoming movie stolen by a rival studio. Certainly, not a case with international import.

"Now, you've *got* to help us, Harry. Can't you see, it's ever so important?" Mary Pickford lifted her face and those famous eyes bored straight into my soul. "Please say you will."

I thought about the consequences if I failed, or if word leaked out about the loss. The press would eat it up, and Miss Pickford and Mr. Fairbanks would be social pariahs for sure. Hollywood loved a good scandal.

I had no choice. "Of course I will, Miss Pickford," I said, with more bravado than I felt. "Don't worry. 'The Hound' can find anything."

That brightened her mood, and she whisked me off to the patio for cocktails and to meet her guests. Exhausted as I was from my journey, the champagne went straight to my head. I wandered around starry-eyed, under the clear Southern California sky, basking in the heady company of Hollywood stars and starlets.

* * * *

The next morning, I rolled out of bed, and spent quite a while enjoying the elaborate shower the couple had installed in my guest suite. I luxuriated in the cascading water, so different from the clawfoot tub back home in my fourth-floor walk-up. Finally, I was ready to get to work.

Miss Pickford had said that our victim hired a maid from a local agency, since her own lady-in-waiting was ill and couldn't make the voyage to California. The replacement's name was Flora, and I decided to hang around the kitchen, on the pretext of looking for a snack and see what gossip I could pick up from the servants.

I didn't have to wait long. Apparently, there's quite a hierarchy between regular house staff and part-timers like Flora.

"Anna, Flora says she needs a cup of tea for her lady, along with a plate of biscuits and she told me to tell you to make it snappy," a short, plump girl who I knew as Polly called out.

"Did she now?" Anna called back, hands on her hips.

"She seems to think she's the royalty, instead of just a hired hand. She should count herself lucky to get the job." Anna didn't look like she was putting on any speed, as she placed the kettle on the stove.

"Well, she certainly has put on airs," Polly said. "Why, I heard her telling one of the other girls just yesterday, that she won't be doing this type of work much longer. Called it 'menial labor' with her nose in the air, she did. Supposedly said she's come into some unexpected wealth."

"Hmph. Wealth. Probably found a sawbuck in milady's coat pocket and now she thinks she's Lady Astor or something." Anna handed over the tea and biscuits with a mocking shake of her head.

"Well, if she does leave, good riddance I say," Polly said as she carried the drink out of the kitchen.

I thanked Anna for my snack, and headed up to the servants' quarters, figuring while Flora was busy with her lady, I'd have a look-see around her room.

There wasn't much to see. A trundle bed covered in a Blue Bonnet quilt, a chair, and a washstand. A simple linen dress hung from the lone hook on the wall, and a trunk stood open, filled with a jumble of clothes, shoes, and some beauty paraphernalia I couldn't identify.

A pocket on the inside of the trunk lid held a sheaf of papers. One was an envelope, addressed to Flora, care of general delivery in Beverly Hills. I tiptoed to the door and had a look up and down the corridor to ensure I wouldn't be surprised by the maid, before perusing the contents.

Turns out our girl Flora really was about to come into some cash, but it wasn't from fencing stolen jewelry. If what this letter said was true, she was soon to have enough money to quit the maid business for good. Seems her uncle, who owned a small factory back East, died recently, leaving no heirs. Flora and her brother stood to inherit the old man's estate. While not a fortune, it was enough to pull the girl out of servitude and into a middle-class life.

* * * *

To keep up the ruse of being an old friend of Miss Pickford's, I had to dress for cocktails and show up in the Wild West bar for before-dinner drinks. It took me a little bit of time to navigate the maze of rooms and find the party, and as I pushed the swinging doors open, it was obvious the shindig was well under way.

I ambled over to the bar, ordered a gin rickey, and leaned back with my foot upon the brass rail to survey my fellow drinkers.

Photoplay wasn't exaggerating the guest lists for the Pickford/Fairbanks soirees. I could see several Hollywood types, familiar from the movies and the newspapers that covered them. The couple's neighbor Rudolph Valentino was there, conferring with Mr. Fairbanks about his plans to renovate the home he had built nearby. Chaplin was there, too, and I was surprised at how short he seemed in person. No wonder they called him "The Little Tramp."

If only my friends from the speakeasy back home could see me now. Especially Clarissa, my favorite barmaid, who dreamed of Hollywood stardom. All the regulars at Art's speakeasy knew the plucky young waitress from Tipperary Hill had dreams of being an actress, and we all hoped we'd see our own "girl with the curls" on the silver screen one day.

Other guests were familiar from the silver screen, too, but in this case, it was the newsreels. Edison held court in one corner, and Lord and Lady Mountbatten made a stunning sight coming through the swinging doors to the saloon.

The rest of the party was rounded out by aspiring actors and actresses, rumpled screenwriters, and people speaking in accents that marked them as visitors from overseas.

I was scanning the room looking for suspicious types, when suddenly I heard loud voices from one corner of the room. A young man, wearing a sweater in the colors of some college or other, waved his glass in the air dramatically as he confronted a man in a tux with a diamond stud in his cravat.

"I tell you they haven't learned a thing after the Wall Street bombing back in '20," the young man shouted. "And don't get me started on the 'Crowned Heads of Europe.' What a holdover from the Middle Ages! Their pride and petty feuds caused millions of lives to be lost or ruined forever in the war, yet they're still at it."

I could hear the other man make a reply but couldn't make out the words of his quietly voiced response.

"Oh, your rich types would think that, but you'll see," said the young man. "The people will take back their property—one case at a time! It's called 'individual reclamation.' And it's happening all over the world."

I watched Mr. Fairbanks go over to the two men and quietly try to defuse the situation. Miss Pickford appeared at my shoulder. "That's Tom Samuels, the son of one of our neighbors. He's home from some university back East, with his head full of revolutionary ideas." She nodded to the bar man, who brought a Mai Tai and set it in front of her. "Don't worry about him. He's mostly hot air."

"I wouldn't be so sure of that," I said as I gestured for a refill to my glass. "He's right about it being a worldwide movement, but some devious types have been stealing valuables in the name of anarchy, only to line their own pockets." I looked over as the three-way conversation moved out into the hall. "It's not always harmless intellectual bluster."

It could well be innocent student blather, but I wanted to keep an eye on Samuels. Stealing the jewels of a royal lady was the sort of move a real anarchist might make. The college boy persona could well hide a committed idealist.

I waited until Mary Pickford drifted away from me to attend to her guests, and then made for the door. I followed Samuels through the hallways of Pickfair until I saw him duck into one of the guest rooms. When he emerged a few minutes later, dressed for dinner, I continued down the hall like I was heading for my own room. As soon as he was out of sight, I doubled back and entered his room.

He kept his room neat, with the varsity sweater he had recently doffed folded and laid on the bed. In his closet were the usual college-boy accoutrements: boater hat, school tie, linen trousers and broughams. A quick search of his drawers and valise turned up no jewels, other than his college ring and a simple tie tack engraved with an S. I scanned the bedside table for reading materials. I found a couple of anarchist fliers, and underneath these was what looked like a term paper, covering the history of the movement. Apparently, our boy was working on a research project for school. A letter from one of his school chums was stuck between the pages of the term paper, reminding him of the upcoming debate in a week's time. It seemed Samuels was a member of a debating team from his fraternity. The subject of the debate? "Resolved: That the workingman deserved to retain the fruits of his labor."

I had to admit Mary was right. Samuels wasn't a rabid revolutionary out to take individual action against the royalty of the world. He was practicing his arguments for the upcoming debate and having a bit of fun at the wealthy guest's expense.

While I was glad to see that the idealistic youngster wasn't the thief, I headed down to dinner a bit dejected. My reputation was at stake, after all. What's more, if our thief were allowed to escape while my investigation was floundering, it could create an international incident and an embarrassing scandal for my clients.

As I passed by the famous inground swimming pool, I could see lights glinting off the water and decided to satisfy my curiosity. Even if The Hound headed back to Syracuse with his tail between his legs, I'd have a story or two to tell about the lifestyle of Hollywood's elite couple.

I took one step into the pool area and stopped in surprise. There was a young woman, sitting and staring into the water. She was holding her head, her blond bob obscuring her hands. I could hear a soft sob, followed by an almost comic sniffle.

I walked back out and entered again, this time making a bit more noise. She lifted her head and I saw it was Lucille, a young actress I'd been introduced to the evening before. I knew she dreamed of stardom, but she hardly looked glamorous now, her eyes red, and her mascara smudged.

"Is everything all right, Lucille?" I asked, approaching the morose girl.

"Oh, Harry, I've been a fool and now I don't know what to do." She turned and stared into the pool, and I followed suit. Just visible in the dark water, I could see something reflecting the electric lights Fairbanks had installed so the pool could be used in the evenings.

I could see a hint of what looked like red, and the sparkle of a million facets.

"Is that what I think it is?" I turned to the ingenue with a shocked look on my face. She nodded and the tears started again.

"I only meant to borrow it. There was a party over at one of the best studios, and all the bigwigs were going to be there. I wanted to make a good impression, show them how successful I'd been, and how beautiful I'd be on the screen." She looked at the water again and shuddered. "On my way back from the party, I was headed to put the bracelet away. But I saw the lady's maid approaching, and I ducked in here, making believe I wanted to cool off at the pool."

She gave her head a rueful shake, her fashionable bob brushing her cheeks. "I figured I'd run my hand leisurely through the water, trying to put on a good act of a lounging beauty, bored with life and relaxing in solitude. But the water made my hand slick and the bracelet slipped off and sank to the bottom of the pool."

Her voice came out in a mere whisper then. "I can't swim, Harry. They'll find me out for sure, and I'll be arrested and sent back to the Midwest in shame." The tears started again. "I only wanted to be a star, not a jailbird."

I gave her a hug then, and as her hair brushed my face and I smelled her delicate perfume, I thought of my friend, Clarissa, and her dreams of Hollywood fame. I felt sad that dreams could so twist a young girl's mind that she'd risk her freedom on a ruse to get ahead in this cutthroat town. I only hoped if Clarissa found herself in a similar pickle, that someone would take pity on her and help her out.

"You're in luck, Lucille, because I *do* know how to swim." Her face lit up at that, and I gave her a wink. "Now you go back to your room and fix up your makeup. Put on your prettiest dress and come sit with me at dinner. Tonight you're going to put on your best performance ever." I eyed her sternly. "I expect you to behave from now on, young lady, and work hard. When I get back East, I want to see your beautiful smile on screen at the movie palaces, and your name on the marquee."

* * * *

"But what did you tell Miss Pickford?" Art asked as he handed me a tumbler of rye, back at the speakeasy in Syracuse.

"I told her the truth. That I wandered into the pool area and saw something glinting at the bottom of her pool. She was so happy to get the bracelet back to its owner, she didn't ask if I knew how it got there." I sipped my drink and sat back with a satisfied sigh.

"Lucille played her part perfectly, and by the end of that evening, I'd introduced her to a director I'd met during the cocktail hour back in the saloon. I received a telegram from her yesterday. She has a part in his new movie, although they're making her take a different stage name. And get this—she's going to play a bathing beauty."

Michele Bazan Reed's stories appeared in *Woman's World* magazine and several anthologies, including "Mayhem on the Cheddar Express" in the Sisters in Crime NY/TriState Chapter anthology, *New York State of Crime: Murder New York Style 6*. A member of SinC's Guppies, Private Eye Writers of America, and Short Mystery Fiction Society, she lives in Central New York, north of Harry's stomping grounds of Syracuse. Like her fictional sleuth, she loves classic film stars.

THE NIGHT BECKHAM BURNED DOWN

ROBERT LOPRESTI

The day Martin LeGrand announced he would be retiring at the end of 1970 a reporter came to interview him. "How does it feel when you solve a really big case, Chief?"

LeGrand thought for a moment and chuckled. "It feels like a fire engine exploding." Then he told this story.

* * * *

The mayor of Beckham appointed me police chief in 1935. That wasn't my original plan, of course. I thought I was going to be a businessman, but after most of a decade of the Great Depression, business hardly existed in Oregon. I became a cop in Portland, and then, when the chief in my hometown passed away, I jumped at the job none of his officers wanted.

The two-hundred-mile drive down the coast was the longest trip I have ever made, because I spent it wondering if I could fill the old chief's shoes, and if people who had known me as a boy could possibly respect me in a uniform. I guess that question really didn't get decided until the next year.

That year—1936—was the hottest, driest summer in the history of Oregon, and on the morning of the last Saturday in September I was sitting in my office, worrying about dance halls. Beckham had three of them and on Saturday nights they filled up with men lucky enough to have jobs and women eager to help them spend their pay. By midnight the fist fights started, and I never had enough officers to cover my bases.

That's what I was thinking about when Jack Bodeen walked into my office. Jack worked in the milk processing plant, and he was a volunteer fireman. I could smell the stink of burning as soon as he walked in. "I've a message from Chief Rogers."

"Take a seat, Jack. What's the problem?"

"The forest fires ain't staying in the hills. If we get an east wind they could come straight into town tonight."

That was a shock. I had known there were fires up there, but that year it seemed like there always were.

"This is the driest day Oregon's ever seen. Up in the woods—" He shook his head. "Pine trees are bursting into flames like hand grenades. The humidity is only eight percent, if you can believe it. When we're lucky enough to have water to pump it evaporates before it hits the fire."

After Jack left, the first thing I did was call Grace Linder, the switchboard operator. She ran the town's phones from an office on top of the bank building. "Start calling everyone on the east side of town, Grace. Warn them the fire in the hills might reach us tonight."

"My lands, Chief. Should they make a run for it?"

"Not yet. But they should be packed and know where they're going if they need to."

"That's a good idea. Think about what to take and what to leave. I'll spread the word, Chief. My lands, what a day."

I sat at my desk, thinking about what Grace had said. If the police station burned, what couldn't I leave behind?

That was easy, so I walked to the two-room jail at the back of the building. Officer Ed Pierce was dishing out lunch. The smell told me it was pot roast from Maggie's Eats, across the street.

"Let him out, Ed."

The officer blinked. He was around forty, a decade older than me. Ed had been a farmer, 'til the bank foreclosed. "You sure, Chief? It took us long enough to catch him."

I looked at our only prisoner: twenty-five years old, shorter than average, and much too skinny for his clothes. Even with big arm muscles he didn't look like much of a threat.

"Arthur Kavalier," I said. "You're a burglar."

"No, sir." His dark brown eyes met mine, straight on. "I'm a carpenter. I'd rather build a house than rob one any day. But nobody's building, and I gotta eat."

"Have you hurt anyone?"

"No, sir. Never laid a hand on man, woman, or child."

I frowned. "You have to promise me something, Arthur. Promise that if I set you free, you'll get out of Beckham and stay out."

"My pleasure, sir." He blinked. "Uh, don't take that the wrong way."

"Just promise me you'll stick to your rule about not hurting anyone."

"I swear it on my mother's grave."

Ed Pierce snorted. "How do we even know she's dead? What's this about, Chief?"

"Looks like the wildfire might pay us a visit tonight. If we have to evacuate downtown, I don't want to have to come back to rescue Mr. Kavalier."

Ed nodded gravely. "I'd as soon not have to risk my life for this boy." He opened the cell.

"Well, thanks, I guess," the burglar said. He hesitated. "Chief, can I finish my lunch first? This is the best meal I've had in months."

* * * *

For the next hour Ed and I mapped a strategy for getting people out of town, if it came to that.

"You should have Mike Paulley take his tug across the river, Chief, and tell the Guard what's up. If the roads get blocked, we'll need to move people by water."

Beckham has grown out to the coast now, but back in the 1930s the business district faced the Chess River, not the Pacific. The Coast Guard had a station on the north shore.

"That's good thinking, Ed. And that little steamboat is over there, too. We may need all the help we can get."

"What about the people who don't have telephones?"

"I'm way ahead of you. Tag and Richie are knocking on doors." Those two officers made up the rest of my force.

The next few hours flew by. The mayor and a bunch of businessmen visited, wanting to know how I was going to save the town. Exactly how the police chief was supposed to do that, they didn't explain. Put the fire in handcuffs, maybe.

It made me wonder, not for the first time, if I was in the right business. Maybe it wasn't too late to get a job with one of the cheese-makers down the coast.

I was all by myself in the middle of the afternoon when Jack Bodeen returned. The fireman had looked worn out before; now he seemed like a man who had gazed into the pits of hell. He didn't bother with hello. "Unless we get a cloudburst the fire will be downtown by midnight. Chief Rogers says everyone east of town should evacuate *now.*"

I remember wishing the mayor had appointed somebody else.

Before I could speak the phone rang. It was Grace, the operator. "Chief, there's a problem."

Only one?

"The phones on Cougar Creek Road are dead. I haven't been able to reach anyone out there."

"So they haven't been warned."

"That's right. And Chief, Mother Hicks lives there."

I covered the phone so Grace wouldn't hear me swear. Maybe you never heard of Mother Hicks. She was as close to a saint as Oregon ever had. Polio put her in a wheelchair when she was a girl, but no one ever heard her complain. The state had no official orphanages back then, so Mother Hicks took in the children of busted-up loggers and lost-at-sea fishermen and cared for them herself, using whatever money she could scrape together.

Naturally she had no car. If the fire came her way—

"The officers are all out," I told Grace. "I'll go myself. Tell anyone you can still reach on the east side to leave *now.* If anyone phones for me, let 'em know I'll be back as soon as I can."

"Be careful, Chief. My lands."

I left a note telling people where I was. Then I climbed in my Packard and headed east.

It was hard to make progress. On every block I was waved over by worried citizens who wanted to know what was happening. I couldn't pass anyone by for fear I'd miss a genuine emergency.

I remember wondering if the old chief I'd replaced would have done this better. How do you keep people's spirits up while telling them to run for their lives?

Cougar Creek Road was where the farms began. Compared to the people milling around downtown this place seemed unnaturally still, like the world holding its breath.

First person I saw was Pete Sodeberg, a farmer, leading a cow along the side of the road. He looked like a man walking an oversized dog.

I pulled over. "Want a ride, Pete?"

The farmer shook his head. "Can't let this old girl burn, Chief. I'll walk her to the river."

"Fast as you can, Pete. Fast as she'll go."

The first house on Cougar Creek Road belonged to Drew McCortland and I found him struggling to strap a white leather suitcase on the roof of a desperately overloaded old Ford. Other household goods lay scattered around him.

"Howdy, Chief. You got room for some of my stuff?"

"I'm just carrying people, Drew. You better get going."

He was a short, middle-aged man. His face wrinkled up like he was about to cry. "Where am I supposed to *go?* I was born in this house, you know. Never been more than sixty miles from here my whole life."

That was McCortland's only boast, and I had heard him make it a thousand times. I always thought it was a strange thing to be proud of.

"Maybe the fire won't come here, Drew, but don't take any chances."

"Oh, I won't, believe you me. This is all *his* fault, you know."

"Who?"

He glared at me. "Roosevelt."

* * * *

I passed the home of Nate and Allene Helmstrom, an elderly couple. I found their son packing them into his pick-up truck, so I waved and kept going.

The next house was boarded up. It probably belonged to someone who had gone to the central valley in search of work. There were plenty of them in those days.

It was getting dark, even though sunset was hours away. Smoke from the hills covered the sky, and it made me desperate to get this done. I wondered if I should skip these houses and make a dash for Mother Hicks's place. It was tempting, but in the end, I couldn't justify it.

The next house seemed to be empty, too. It belonged to Mrs. Woods, an elderly woman who had moved to Beckham two years before.

There was no answer at the door. I moved down the porch and peered in a window at a neat, sparsely furnished living room. There was no one in sight.

Did someone come to her rescue? She had told everyone that her only relative was a nephew in California. According to Mrs. Woods, the young man made a lot of money in the movie business, but seldom wrote to his poor old aunt and never sent her a penny.

The front door was unlocked, so I knocked again and went in.

"Mrs. Woods?"

Three suitcases and an old-fashioned hat box sat at the foot of the stairs. All packed up, ready to go.

She was in the kitchen, lying in a pool of blood. Someone had bashed her head with a clothes iron.

That made me dizzy. I had seen dead bodies before. Loggers who sliced through their cables while trimming the tops. Drunkards who lost meaningless bar room battles.

But this was a first time I'd seen someone purposely killed. Without thinking, I reached for the phone. It was dead, of course.

It took a moment to get my brain into gear. Then I did a quick search to make sure the killer wasn't in the house. The next step was to secure the crime scene. But how do you do that when the whole place might burn overnight?

I ran upstairs and yanked the quilt off Mrs. Woods' bed. I wrapped the poor woman in it. It was awkward, but fortunately she was small and light. I remember apologizing to her, although I don't think I spoke out loud.

Getting her into the trunk of the Packard was harder. I couldn't spare the backseat, not if I hoped to fit Mother Hicks' brood inside.

Next was Pete Sodeberg's farm. I didn't have to stop there, since I had already seen him, walking his cow.

And speaking of pedestrians, there was someone standing on the road. He had stopped to adjust a big pillowcase he was carrying.

It was Arthur Kavalier.

I've heard the expression *seeing red* a thousand times, but that was the only time I ever experienced it. I was so mad my vision faded to a scarlet blur. *He killed that poor old woman. I let him out of jail, and he robbed her and murdered her.*

Kavalier didn't know it was me in the car. He just stood watching as I stopped, and he was still there when I jumped out, reaching for my gun. That's when he started to run, west through Sodeberg's fields.

"You stop or I'll shoot!" I shouted.

He kept going.

I raised my pistol in both hands and took careful aim. It was the first time I'd ever fired in the line of duty.

The bullet tore a hole in Kavalier's pillowcase. It hit glass and made a hell of a noise.

"My God!" he yelled. He dropped the pillowcase like it bit him and raised his hands over his head.

"Don't move," I said, walking toward him.

"I just stole a few doodads that were gonna burn anyway. I can't believe you'd kill someone over that."

"I can't believe *you* would. That you *did.*" I put the handcuffs on him. "Turn around."

Kavalier frowned. "What are you talking about? I didn't kill anyone."

"Don't try it. I have her body in the trunk of my car. You have her stuff in that sack, and I saw you walking away from her house."

He shook his head. "I don't know who you're talking about, but I was heading *south,* the direction you were coming from. So, whoever was behind you is nothing to do with me."

I thought about it. When I first saw Kavalier he had been standing still and facing sideways. There was no way to know which direction he had been coming from.

I picked up the pillowcase. "Back to my car. Hurry up."

"You really got a dead woman in the trunk?"

I hustled him to the Packard and opened the door. "Get in."

But Kavalier yanked his arm free. He was looking down the road, eyes wide. "What the hell is *that?*"

The road bent a quarter of a mile ahead and all you could see beyond that was pine trees. But something was coming out of the woods, straight toward us.

It was the damnedest thing I've ever seen. Ever see one of those cartoons where fire takes on a human shape and starts running around? That's what this looked like. Except this fire was an animal, heading straight toward us on four burning legs. And it was real.

"It's a deer," I told Kavalier. "On fire. Get in the car."

The carpenter backed away. "No, sir. There's no time."

"Damn it, get in!"

But he was running away, handcuffs and all, back over the fields.

The deer collapsed on the road ten yards from my car, a burning, stinking mess. Now I could see the main fire behind it, moving through the woods toward the road. Kavalier was right; there was no time to start the car and turn it around.

I followed him into the fields, shouting: "Go left!"

He was smart enough to follow orders. I led him to Sodeberg's cranberry bog. Even in this dry weather there were still a few inches of water in the bottom of the pond. As I slid down the hill and threw myself in, I could hear Kavalier crashing down the slope on my right. I shouted for him to get in the water.

The flames were right behind us. It felt like I was sitting in a roaring fireplace, and I thought the hairs on the back of my head might burst into flame. I took a deep breath of hot dry air and threw myself backward into the bog.

The water was warm and slimy, but it was a bubble bath compared to what was above us. I felt the firestorm passing over the muck. The water trembled like a mighty tide was flowing through the little bog. I tried to track the seconds but all I could count were the thumping beats of my heart, going faster than the hands of any clock.

I stayed down until my chest was ready to burst. Finally, I had to push to the surface and gasp for air, hoping I wouldn't breathe in a mouthful of lung-destroying fire instead.

It was air, all right. Hot, bone-dry, and stinking of ash, but I could breathe it.

Sodeberg's neat field was a blackened wasteland, the few trees unrecognizable skeletons. And the fire was still moving toward town.

I heard desperate struggle. Kavalier, in handcuffs, was trying to get his face above water. I grabbed his arm and dragged him to the surface. He gasped and groaned.

"On your feet."

He flopped around like a beached fish. "You—you saved my life."

"Didn't want you to cheat the hangman." I pulled him up by the shoulder.

"I don't know what you saw back there, Chief, but I swear to God I never touched a soul. I robbed an empty house."

"Is that right? Let's get back to the car and I'll show you the body. See if you can lie in front of the evidence. Then—Damn it!"

A sharp pain almost knocked me over.

"Chief?"

"I must have twisted my ankle sliding down." I looked up the hill, which now seemed longer and higher.

"Lean on me."

I looked at my prisoner. Was he planning to grab my gun with his cuffed hands? Or at least knock me over and make a run for it?

"It's up to you, Chief. But we won't get anywhere at the speed you're walking."

I scaled the hill by myself, using my hands to struggle up the steeper bits. That's when I realized how bad our situation really was.

My Packard had exploded. I hadn't even heard it, being underwater at the time. It was a smoldering wreck. The trunk, where I had put Mrs. Woods for safekeeping, was a twisted heap of metal.

"Oh, brother," Kavalier said. "Was that your own car? What a tough break."

If he was putting on a show, he was good at it. Maybe he didn't realize that the evidence of his crime had just gone up in flame.

It also occurred to me that if Kavalier had followed my order and climbed into the car, we would both be dead now.

I took off the handcuffs. "You're still under arrest. But I'm gonna need your help to get back to town."

"Sure, Chief."

"You try anything funny, I swear I'll shoot you."

He blinked. "I'll keep that in mind."

From the rise I could see that a whim of the fire had left Yamhill Road, west of the Sodeberg farm, untouched. It took us almost an hour to cross the scorched fields to get there. I kept hoping to find a stick I could use as a cane, but everything made of wood had burned to ash. I leaned on Kavalier. We circled places where the ground was too hot to walk.

Halfway across the field I realized that my clothes, drenched in the cranberry bog, were bone-dry again. That's how dry the air was.

By then the sun was about to set.

When we reached the road, our luck changed. A flatbed truck came up almost immediately. The driver was Sam Pargood, a boat-builder who lived north of the river. His wife Maggie and their two kids were wedged in the cab beside him.

"Can you give us a ride to town, Sam?"

He looked troubled. "I don't know, Chief. We were heading up to my house."

"This is official business."

"It's not the detour I mind. Take a look at my cargo."

I did a double take. I had been so intent on Sam I hadn't even noticed that his flatbed was covered with children. And in the middle, like a queen on her throne, was Mother Hicks. She sat in her big, old-fashioned wheelchair, peaceful as if they were headed to a church picnic.

"Evening, Chief. Warm enough for you?" Some of the kids laughed. You had to admire her, keeping them calm in a situation where many adults would panic.

Sam was out of the cab, running a worried hand through his red hair. "Sammy Jr. was playing at their house when we heard about the fire, so we rushed over. I don't know, Chief. Maybe we could fit one of you on the bed, but there ain't any way to squeeze in two."

"You've got the bum leg," Kavalier said. "I'll walk."

I looked at him. Was this a murderer trying to escape?

No. This was an unemployed carpenter risking his life to help the man who was trying to send him to prison.

That's when I lost faith in the brilliant deduction I made when I spotted him on the road. Whoever killed Mrs. Woods, it wasn't him.

"You go," I told him. "I'll be okay."

"What a pack of fools," Mother Hicks said. We turned to stare at her.

"*Nobody's* getting left behind. There's plenty of room in the lifeboat." She made a fancy wave at the truck with one hand. "Scott, Timmy, help me out of this thing."

The two oldest boys lifted her out of the wheelchair. She grimaced as her twisted legs hit the truck bed.

"Now, throw it overboard." The boys pushed the wheelchair off. It crashed into the ditch on the side of the road and one girl started to cry.

"Come here, Pamela," Mother Hicks said, and pulled the little one to her heart. "We can always replace *things,* honey. It's *people* we gotta take care of. Let's go, gentlemen."

She was right. Without the big wheelchair we could squeeze on. I climbed up, but Kavalier stood facing Mother Hicks and I'm darned if he didn't salute.

"Permission to come aboard your lifeboat, Captain."

As sure as I'm sitting here, she saluted right back. "Granted. Shake a leg."

We rolled then, and I remember thinking that there was no way we could have fit all these kids in my car even if it hadn't burned. It was a miracle Sam had come to the rescue.

We found Tag Penitten, one of my officers in his patrol car, blocking off the last road into town. His eyes went wide as hub caps when he saw me sitting on the edge of that truck with all those kids. "The fire's spreading. Chief Rogers went into the theatre and stopped the movie. Told people to get out of town or help fight the fire."

"Any way we can get back in?"

"Go across the river. The Coast Guard is ferrying people."

I nodded. "That's where Sam is headed. Find something to block this road, Tag, and head that way yourself. I don't want you here if the fire comes."

That was one man I'd made happy today. "Yes, sir."

Sam left me and my prisoner off on the north side of the Chess River. That was quite a sight. Every vessel for miles around was ferrying people away from Beckham. There was a small steamboat, a lumber schooner, a whole bunch of rowboats. It reminded me of pictures of refugees in World War I.

I looked at Kavalier. "I suppose I should handcuff you to something. Make sure you don't run for it."

The carpenter shook his head. "You need every hand you can find, Chief. Putting cuffs on two of them doesn't make sense. I'll stay and help folks. You can lock me up in the morning if the jail doesn't burn down first."

Some of the buildings at the far end of Front Street were already in flame. "That's a big if."

When I reached the pier, a fisherman named Max Jaffee was helping a shell-shocked family out of his boat. "Sure, I'll take you across, Chief. Ain't nobody else looking for a trip back. Damnedest thing I've ever seen."

As we motored across the river it looked like half the town of Beckham was crowded on the south beach, facing downtown as it burned. They had driven their cars onto the sand as far as they could, hoping to save them from the fire, but as we landed sparks from a burning building rained down on one old truck and set it ablaze.

I spotted Officer Ed Pierce leading a bucket brigade, not having much luck. As I hobbled out of Max's boat a big family started climbing in the other side.

Max gave me a broken oar to use as a cane and I staggered up the beach. By the light of the fire I could see Pete Sodeberg, trying to calm his cow. By God, they made it. And I spotted Drew McCortland, the man who blamed the fire on Roosevelt, waiting in line for the next boat.

Pierce's eyes widened when he saw me. "Chief! You're okay!"

"More or less, Ed. How bad is it?"

"We've lost most everything south of Eugene Street. They had to carry Grace Linder out of the bank building."

"Was she hurt?"

"Nope. She wouldn't desert the switchboard, even though most of the phone lines were fried."

"Brother. So, the police station is gone."

"That's right. Chief, you were right to free that thief. Otherwise, he'd be dead now."

I made a face. "Listen, Ed. You remember Mrs. Woods?" I told him what had happened.

"I'll be damned. You left a thief and murderer to play around with all those people on the other side of the river?"

"I don't think he's a killer, Ed."

"A burglar then. Well, that's great. What harm can he do, surrounded by people trying to hold onto their last few possessions?"

"You want me to bring him over here so you can watch him?"

Pierce shrugged. "You could have taken him to the Coast Guard station. They must have a brig, or something."

He was right so I didn't argue. Instead, I headed over to Ike Rogers, the fire chief, who was standing next to a fire engine on Front Street. Two of his men held the engine's hose as it poured a small sad stream of water onto the remains of the Mercantile Store.

Rogers was a big, barrel-chested man, and he looked mad enough to chew nails. "We're losing downtown, Chief. Concrete buildings are folding up. Fire hoses are *melting*. I'm calling my boys out before one of them gets killed."

"Do what you have to do, Chief. I wish— Man!"

The movie theatre dropped in a shuddering heap, sending out a storm of ashes that rained down on us. We dodged as best we could and then the chief saw something I missed.

Sparks had landed on the fire engine, and it was starting to smoke. Rogers yelled at the top of his voice. "Jack! Get off *now!*"

Fireman Jack Bodeen was standing on top of the engine, with his back to the blaze. He took one look behind him and dived off the other side.

He'll break his neck, I thought. But I had forgotten that Front Street was built right along the riverbank at that point, and Jack landed in shallow water. He came up spitting mud, but unharmed.

That's when the fire engine exploded. The boom sent out a shockwave that scorched what was left of my hair.

As I hit the pavement, I instinctively turned to see if anyone was hurt. By the crazy firelight I could see people all the way across the beach, ducking down, hiding behind their belongings, each other, any shelter they could find.

All except for Drew McCortland, that is. He ducked, all right, but instead of trying to hide behind his big white suitcase, he was kneeling in front of it, trying to protect it with his body.

It was then, right then, I knew that being a policeman was what I wanted to do for the rest of my life.

I walked across the beach, not even using my makeshift cane.

"How you doing, Drew?"

The little man glared at me. "I'd be better if anyone in this town knew their jobs. Why can't the cops and the fire department *protect* us?"

"Good question. Now here's one for you. Where'd you get that beautiful suitcase?'

McCortland looked at the white leather suitcase and back at me. "At a time like this you're want to know where I bought my *luggage?* Are you crazy?"

The fact is, I felt a little nuts. "When I passed your house before, that suitcase was the last thing you were packing on top of your car. You left it for last, and yet it's the one thing you chose to bring on the boat. Kind of odd, don't you think?"

He was tight-lipped. "You must have something better to do than ask me dumb questions, Chief."

"I don't think it's dumb, Drew. I mean, that's really a fine piece of leather. I'd be surprised if any store closer than Portland sold something like that."

He looked at the case like he was seeing it for the first time. "Maybe so."

"But you've never been to Portland, right? Because that's more than sixty miles from Beckham."

He blinked. "That's right, Chief. I bought it from a hobo passing through town."

Well, that was possible. In the middle of the Depression, you might find anybody selling darned near anything. But I didn't believe it.

McCortland started to bluster. "Don't you have better things to do than ask about my baggage, Chief?"

"You know something, Drew? I don't think I do. In fact, I don't think I have ever wanted anything in my whole life as much as I want to see what's in that suitcase of yours."

He scowled. "Well, that's too bad, ain't it? I thought this was still a free country, in spite of Mr. Roosevelt. Don'tcha need a warrant, or something?"

"I suppose I do, if you won't let me take a peek. But as you said, I'm in charge of protecting people, so I don't need a warrant to do this." I turned to the others in line, waiting for a boat.

"Hey folks, this is Drew McCortland. He's a farmer and I happen to know he uses dynamite to blow out tree stumps. I think he might have some in that suitcase."

McCortland stared at me. "I do not!"

One of the men in line had his wife and three kids with them. His face went red with rage. "Dynamite? Are you out of your *mind?* Have you noticed the whole damn town's on fire?"

McCortland backed away, hugging the big case to his chest. "There's no dynamite, Walt, I swear it."

"Then show us what's in it," someone shouted.

I took him by the arm. "It's okay, folks. I'll take care of it."

When we were a safe distance from the crowd, I let go of McCortland. "There you have it, Drew. I don't think they'll let you get in a boat without seeing what you've got in there."

The little man was speechless. He stared at me, at the burning buildings, and finally at the rescue boat that was pulling up to the shore.

All of a sudden, he sat down on the suitcase and began to cry. "Doggone it. It just goes to show, no good deed goes unpunished."

I frowned. "Bashing an old woman's head was your good deed for the day?"

McCortland looked up at me. His face, like everyone else's, was dark with ash and dust, but now there were clean streaks where his tears had poured. "That wasn't the idea. I went there to help her. She had no car and no way to get out. I told her to get one bag ready and I'd be back in ten minutes.

"When I got back Mrs. Woods had half a dozen suitcases lined up and she started giving me orders like I was her servant instead of her goddamn rescuer. I saw what was in here—" he patted the white bag. "I told her I was gonna charge her twenty dollars for the ride to town. Hell, I was leaving stuff worth more than that behind to make room for her. But she was so damned stubborn, Chief. Stood there with her arms folded, refusing to pay a cent. I either had to take her for free or leave her to burn. I thought, maybe I could knock her out and carry her. Then I saw the iron and—well."

"You killed her."

"Yeah." He looked down at the beach. "Yeah, I did."

"So, what's in the suitcase, Drew?"

McCortland stood up. "You don't know? Take a look."

I opened the suitcase and stared at more money than I'd ever seen outside of a bank. When we counted it later it turned out to be a bit over five thousand dollars. More than two years' salary for me.

"Can you blame me?" McCortland said in a cracked, high voice.

"Turn around, Drew. You're under arrest."

I called Ed Pierce over and told him to escort McCortland across to the Coast Guard station and find a place to lock him up. "He's the killer, huh?" said Ed. "Well, I'll be danged."

"Who's a killer?"

I turned around and saw a fat man fumbling with an old-fashioned camera. It was Herb Casey, the publisher of the *Beckham Beacon*. I waved for Ed to take the prisoner off.

"That was Drew McCortland, Herb. He killed old Mrs. Woods."

"Killed?" The publisher looked up, dropping a flashgun. "You mean hit her with a car, or a real murder?"

"Real murder."

"Oh, my word. Talk about feast or famine." He looked at the camera and at the figures disappearing into a boat. He sighed. "I'm hopeless with this thing. My photographer is in Coos Bay, covering a fair. I can't *believe* this. First real murder this town has ever had, and I may not even have room for it in the paper."

I stared at him. "What paper are you talking about? Your office went up in flames ten minutes ago."

Casey shrugged. "Not important, Chief. One of the other papers will lend me space until I get on my feet again. Probably the *Sentinel.*"

"But you hate the *Sentinel.* You and that publisher write terrible things about each other."

"Doesn't matter. Journalists stick together in a crisis. The Fourth Estate is a sacred brotherhood. Besides," he added, more quietly, "your own printing press might be the next one to break down.

"But the first issue we put out will be a four-page extra and I don't know if I can squeeze a little murder into it. We have to do justice to our most important story, and I already know how the headline will read."

"Beckham Burns Down?"

"No, Chief." He smiled. *"Beckham Must Rebuild!"*

"And that's just how the headline read," LeGrand said.

"I see it every day," the reporter said. "That front page hangs in a frame in our newsroom."

"Herb and our mayor worked like madmen that fall. They convinced a dozen county and state officials to write to the president, explaining that Oregon couldn't recover from the Depression without a strong city on the Chess River. So, Roosevelt found some money to help."

"I'm proud my paper was part of it. Did they hang McCortland?"

"No. There wasn't enough left of Mrs. Woods for the coroner to confirm how she died. He had twelve other bodies to worry about that week, all dead in the fire. The district attorney was nervous about trying Drew for murder with only my testimony as evidence. He convinced him to plead guilty to robbery, which we *could* prove."

"And what about the money?"

"Oh yes, the money." LeGrand smiled. "Remember I said Mrs. Woods used to complain that her no-good nephew made it rich in Hollywood and never sent her a penny? The post office—which *didn't* burn—had his address. Seems he'd been writing to her every week.

"And that's where the money came from. The nephew had been sending it to her all that time and she'd been squirreling it away, while telling everyone what a rat he was for deserting her."

LeGrand shrugged. "Today I suppose we'd say she was mentally ill. Back then we said she was a mean-spirited old miser."

"Maybe both," suggested the reporter.

"Could be. So, imagine how that poor nephew felt when he came up here to bury his dear murdered aunt and discovered she'd been bad-mouthing him to everyone she met. I guess being called a cheapskate stuck in his craw because he insisted on paying for the funeral from his own pocket and wouldn't take a red cent from that suitcase.

"'I sent the money for her to live on,' he said. 'I never meant to see it again. Chief, give it to the family in town that needs and deserves it the most.'"

"So how did you choose the family?" asked the reporter.

"That was easy." LeGrand smiled again. "The first thing Mother Hicks did was buy herself a nice new wheelchair. She used the rest of the money to build a house big enough for all her orphans and more. Of course, with construction going on all over town, it was hard for her to find a good carpenter. But I knew one who felt he owed me a favor."

"Arthur Kavalier."

"Correct. He and Mother Hicks got along so well that he stayed on as her handyman. He lived here in Beckham until Pearl Harbor, when he joined the Navy."

LeGrand sighed. "Kavalier died in a Japanese POW camp in November 1944. But he lived one month longer than Drew McCortland, who lost a knife fight in the prison yard. If there's a moral there, you'll have to find it for yourself."

✗

AUTHOR'S NOTE

There is no town named Beckham in Oregon, but there is Bandon. Curt Beckham wrote a wonderful little book named The Night Bandon Burned, *and much of what I describe—the deer, the bog, the wheelchair, the fire engine—really happened that awful night in 1936. I simply inflicted the events on a much-compressed cast of (fictional) characters and added a robbery and a murder. There was a "miser" who died in the fire, and her slandered nephew did refuse the hoarded money.*

Robert Lopresti is a retired librarian who lives in Washington State. His 100-plus stories have been published in most of the mystery magazines and been reprinted in *The Best American Mystery Stories.* He recently edited *Crimes Against Nature: New Stories of Environmental Villainy.*

THE HOTEL RAIDS
MATTHEW WILSON

Hans Burg hated the hotel raids, but he would tell himself there was always something unpleasant about every kind of job.

Take the butcher, for example. He had plenty of plenty of *Wurst* for himself, even in those first years after the war. But the butcher had to hate the smell of pig's intestines, or the slick animal fat he couldn't quite wash off after a day's work.

Or the baker. Sweet strudels and tortes, those were the pleasant benefits of a life covered in flour. And the warmth of the oven in the dead of winter. Who wouldn't take that over laying bricks with fingers frozen around a trowel? But the hours. Burg had a favorite bakery, and he was acquainted with the baker, Herr Kraus, but he didn't envy his job. Kraus was up every night waiting for the yeast to rise while the rest of the world slept, and that same world was at his door every morning expecting fresh bread—rye and wheat and pumpernickel.

Burg's job as a cop, a *Schupo*, had its good side. A regular pay day, which was hard to find in those years after the war. Little gifts to purchase a policeman's blind eye—cigarettes and whiskey and butter could buy his ignorance, especially concerning Bad Kissingen's thriving black market. And he didn't mind delivering a drunk husband to his wife's door or clearing an unsightly vagrant from the spa district. But the hotel raids, they were the butcher's grease, the baker's nightshift.

* * * *

Burg and three other *Schupos* would get the pass key from the innkeeper, creep up the stairs, and enter rooms without knocking. These were small hotels, a few private rooms over a tavern. They would shove the pass key into the locks, shout "*Polizei*" and swing the doors open, where they would find women and girls, undressed or on their way, and young men from far away, GIs from Oklahoma and Chicago—some called them cowboys and gangsters. Burg would deliver the GIs to Daley Barracks, where he imagined they were punished with winks and envy. The women and girls, the *Veronikas*, Burg took them away to court.

Tuesday, and it was the same routine. Burg worked the key and Schmidt pushed through the first door. What did they find? A blonde in a slip twisting her arms to unhook her brassiere from behind. A man in boxers reclining on the bed.

The man bolted up, speaking in quick English. "What the hell is going on? Wait just a minute…"

Schmidt shoved his ID at him, saying "*Polizei*," his voice full of disinterest. The woman crouched to the floor, her hands searching for her skirt and blouse.

This moment of the raids bothered Burg the most. A blonde in her underclothes, and he knew he liked to look. He had his desires, after all. It was hard *not* to look. And the woman was a nice shape, not so thin the way they all looked right after the war when there was no bread on the shelves. But the whole business gave him a bellyache, as if he had swallowed a *Semmel Knödel* without chewing, the dumpling lying there like a ball in his stomach.

The man in boxers looked as if he never missed a meal, and Burg could see it in the extra skin hanging over the lip of his waistband. But all these *Amis* looked well fed. In that mess hall of theirs at Daley Barracks they could get Texas beef, fried pork chops, green beans from enormous cans.

"Listen gentlemen," the *Ami* said, "this is a big misunderstanding. This here is my fiancé. We're scheduled to get married at the post chapel next week. We got ahead of ourselves, that's all."

Schmidt said, "Nevertheless, by order of the court…put your clothes on, Herr…"

"Sergeant…Sergeant Jones."

"Sergeant Jones, very well. The clothes first, and then we can proceed from there."

The blonde pulled her skirt up and zipped it, then swung an arm into the sleeve of her blouse. Sergeant Jones moved slowly, showing a reluctance to surrender. He was not used to taking orders from Kraut cops. But when he finally made his move for his trousers, Burg knew his resistance was over.

In the next room they found a redhead sitting in the bed and tucking the sheets under her arms to cover herself.

"*Polizei*," Schmidt said, the ID coming out again.

The redhead sucked in her breath, and a theatrical shock spread across her face. An act, Burg thought, as he checked the window while Schmidt stepped over to the wardrobe. Schmidt pulled at the doors, and out came a man who was clearly not the redhead's German husband. This GI was dark and minus the boxers.

"By order of the court," Schmidt said, and Burg couldn't help but think Schmidt was some kind of machine, so mechanical in his actions, a bit heartless. He would make a good executioner. Burg glanced at the woman, whose freckled arms pulled tightly at the bed covers. She would be in for some trouble, that was for sure, more trouble than she knew.

By the third room there were no more surprises. Burg and Schmidt found an *Ami* sitting on the bed shirtless, a cigarette pinched in his lips.

"Gentlemen," he said, "you've made a mistake here." Schmidt pulled out his ID, but this *Ami* was having none of it. He was an officer, a captain, and he flaunted his nonchalance, the privilege of the officer class. Schmidt and Burg had seen it before. The Captain's date for the night, Burg would discover, was one from the platoon of *Fräuleins* whose quick typing and good English landed them prized spots in the *Amis'* secretarial pool. She was stroking her hair with a brush at the dressing table as if nothing were the matter.

Leaving the captain and secretary to their evening, Burg and Schmidt retreated to the hallway, Schmidt turning to Burg and saying, "Two out of three, that will have to do for tonight."

* * * *

At the station they had no cells for women, so Schmidt planted the blonde and the redhead in chairs and made them sit there all night.

Burg offered cigarettes and said, "You're lucky it's a Tuesday. If it were a Friday, you would be here until Monday. You don't want to go up against Judge Schubert on a Monday morning after missing three night's sleep. Better a Wednesday morning with only one night lost."

The blonde frowned at this advice.

"Take my word for it, don't put that face on tomorrow. Show a sad face instead. Fear is good, too. When Judge Schubert questions you, look ashamed, even if you're not, and maybe he will go light on you."

"What I want to know," the redhead said, "is how you knew we were up there? Of all the places in town…"

Burg put a finger to his lips and made a shush sound. "Police secrets. We have our methods…but I'll give you some advice for the future. Park a big red Ford right outside a cheap hotel, and you're sure to see trouble."

"That didn't belong to either of our men."

"The officer in the third room," Burg said. "Only the *Amis* would show off their money like that."

"Why pick on us? It's not like you don't have worse troubles. Do you have to go banging into a girl's room in the middle of the night?"

"Haven't you heard? There's a new crisis in Germany. In Baumholder they have fifty-thousand GIs…and night clubs and *Veronikas* for every one of them. Loud music and rowdy brawls—no one wants that here in Bad Kissingen. Every mother is afraid her own daughter might get snatched off the street…or more likely, go willingly. The council in Baumholder has declared it a 'moral disaster area.' They're afraid the *Amis* are going to corrupt our entire youth. The girls…well, you know how that goes…and the boys, they want to be like the *Amis*. But not here in Bad Kissingen if Judge Schubert can help it."

Burg pointed over at Schmidt, who was bent over a typewriter. "Schmidt says the *Amis* laugh too loud, call every girl '*Schatze*' and every man 'pal.'

And before long they'll have our children saying '*Du*' to every person they meet, even Judge Schubert."

The redhead laughed, amused by the idea of the informal *you* for everyone, even stuffy old judges.

Burg grinned and said, "Don't even think about it. Like I said, your best chance is to go in there as if you've just come from confession and you're ready to repent, even if you don't mean it."

* * * *

Burg thought Judge Schubert was so stiff he probably used the formal "*Sie*" with his own wife. Instead of "*Ich liebe Dich*," it was "*Ich liebe Sie.*" Boy, that sounded strange. And what kind of love would that be from this man who had made it his duty to split up lovers?

Ever since the mess in Baumholder, all the garrison towns in Bavaria were trying to clean up. The church sent priests to admonish landlords who rented rooms to single women. "Don't turn your home into a den of vice. Be on the lookout for male visitors—and especially the Negro soldiers." And in Schubert's courtroom it seemed there was no such thing as true love between an *Ami* and a German girl. All the girlfriends and fiancées and "soldier's brides" were *Veronikas* in Schubert's estimation.

Veronika—the *Amis* came up with the term, and even Judge Schubert couldn't help but use it. Since the end of the war, the *Amis'* presence had grown to nearly overpower German life—music, cinema, clothing, and now even the language. *Veronika* started as a joke, from the films they showed the soldiers about taking care when they were out in the streets and nightclubs, to watch out for prostitutes, for V.D. *Veronika, Danke Schön.* An *Ami* Burg knew had explained it to him. He wondered if Schubert had any clue of the term's origin.

In the court Wednesday morning Schubert gave those girls the heavy hand, determined to break the spell of *Amerikanismus.*

"Is a ride in a shiny Cadillac enough to trade your virtue? The *Amis* can give you lipstick and nylon stockings, they can turn you on a dance floor, but they will never give you a proper home."

The girls hung their heads. They had no attorney to defend them, only a social worker, a woman who could be their mother. Schubert lectured on, and Burg detected echoes of the recently failed Reich, when men harped on *Kinder, Kirche, Kuche*—children, church, and kitchen. A woman's place. But women today had another choice, and they found it in the occupation, where free and easy GIs had money to spare and didn't ask for much beyond a good time.

Schubert ranted about widespread indecency, cultural pollution, vulgar consumerism, illegitimate cohabitation, and "secret prostitution," where a nice girl's night out with a corporal ended with gifts—twenty marks or a few packs of cigarettes.

That windbag could blow.

When Schubert moved on to his interrogation, he started with the blonde.

"So, this man of yours, Sergeant Jones, he has proposed marriage to you?"

"Yes, Herr Schubert." She had her hands crossed over her tummy and she had combed down her hair, her permanent wave tamed by vigorous brush strokes.

"*Fräulein*, do you know how many girls come into my courtroom with tales of impending weddings? Do you really believe this sergeant will marry you? In a year's time he will be on a ship back to America, and you will be looking for your next sugar daddy."

The social worker began to protest, but Schubert cut her off.

"It is the common practice of these *Veronikas* to move from one man to the next. Last week I had a girl in here who had lived with three men in the span of a year. Once the first soldier boy stopped bringing her new shoes, she moved on to the next, and then a third. And they were all 'fiancées.'"

He paused and took a drink of water, as if he were playing at tennis and he needed refreshment between sets.

"Now, *Fräulein*, tell me of your relationship with your so-called fiancée... and leave no detail to spare."

The blonde proceeded to explain how the charming sergeant was a gentleman who brought her flowers and held doors for her, and how their affection was authentic and not a convenient arrangement.

"I love Sergeant Jones, and he loves me," she said.

Schubert sighed. "But certainly this match has satisfied other desires... beyond love."

The blonde began to protest, but the social worker gripped her by the elbow.

"Material desires," Schubert said, "...physical desires."

Then he made her tell it. The sergeant's seduction, the details of their intimacy. Where, when, how, how often. Burg watched the social worker object. Wasn't it enough that they pulled this girl from her bed half-clothed? But Schubert insisted. And when he was done, he wanted an inventory. The nylons she wore in court, the permanent wave she had hidden so poorly. And eggs and butter and coffee. Had she traded the sergeant's Lucky Strikes for her groceries, her *Lebensmittel*?

The blonde cowered, as if her head could dip no further in shame. Schubert turned his attention to the redhead.

"Tell me, *Fräulein*, is it the music the Negroes play, is that what drives you to run around in such a notorious fashion?"

Burg had a sense about this one. She was different. She *was* following his advice—head down, a posture of surrender—but when she didn't respond immediately to Schubert's questioning, he worried this would go badly. Schubert prodded her as he had the blonde, to tell the intimate details of her relationship with the dark GI who had been found hiding in the wardrobe, but she stood silent.

Schubert banged down his fist. "Defiance! I won't have it. Answer the court's questions!"

After a long moment, the redhead pulled up her chin and stared at him.

"Well?" Schubert said.

"You're nothing but a worthless, dirty old man. Like all the other old men still hanging around. All the good ones died in the war… You can go to hell, Herr Schubert!"

Schubert declared both women in violation of the criminal code outlawing prostitution in communities smaller than 20,000, saying, "*Fräuleins*, what you can do in Frankfurt, you cannot do in Bad Kissingen."

He gave the blonde a month in jail and sent the redhead to the workhouse for two years. Leaving the court, Burg had "*Du*" ringing in his ears. Twice the redhead had done it, calling Schubert "*Du*" with all the familiar hatred she could muster.

* * * *

In his heart Hans Burg hoped the redhead hadn't counted him in her number of worthless old men. True, he was one of those still alive after the war, though he came close enough to dying too many times for him to want to remember. But he was only thirty-two, not an old man yet.

When he rolled into Poland in '39, he was nineteen. The next five years were nothing but death, and all he wanted was life. When the *Amis* took him prisoner in France in '44, he was relieved. Somehow, he had not died. He was not so unlucky as four million other German men—"the good ones," the redhead had called them, but Burg only thought of them as "the dead ones."

At Eberman's Keller that evening, he told the story of the redhead to the regulars, other men like him who had not died in the war, though Rudy left a foot in the Ukraine thanks to a Russian mine, and Ernst wore an eyepatch, the result of shrapnel in the Ardennes.

Karl-Heinz said, "I don't think her big mouth mattered much. It was the Negro. Schubert always goes harder on the girls caught with Negroes. It's always to the workhouse for girls with Negroes."

Rudy said, "But two years? One year, sure, but two? That had to be for her big mouth."

"I tried to warn her," Burg said.

"A girl who would go to bed with a Negro, there's no controlling her. It's no wonder your advice went unheeded." This was the barman. They called him Papa, though he was only ten years older than Burg. He swept empties off the deck and poured fresh ones.

Ernst said, "Do you think the *Amis* will ever go home? It's been seven years now."

"Not soon. But it's either the *Amis* or the Russians," Rudy said, "and we all know which ones we prefer."

"At least they aren't shooting at each other."

"Like Korea?"

Burg said, "Some of the *Amis* I talk to, they've been to that war, and let me tell you, they're happy to be in Germany."

"Of course they are," Papa said. "They get the pick of our women and it's four marks to the dollar. With those odds, my son can't even get a date with the homeliest girl in town."

"So then Schubert's work is good for your boy?" This was Karl-Heinz.

"Good for my boy, and your daughter, too. How old is she now? Sixteen? Give Schubert another year and he will make Bad Kissingen safe enough for my son to take your daughter out."

There was a burst of laughter, but Burg didn't join it. "I don't see how putting girls in jail is going to help either one of your children."

The men fell silent. They all knew Burg spoke the truth. Life was getting better in Germany. The *Amis* brought the Marshall Plan, so a man might find a job building a road or working in a factory. The coal shortages in the winter seemed a thing of the past. And Volkswagen was already exporting the Beetle, even to America. But still, men like Burg and Karl-Heinz couldn't afford the 4,000 marks to buy one. Meanwhile the *Amis* showed signs of a long-term stay. Burg could see it in their cars—not the drab, utilitarian jeeps—but the private cars the *Amis* began shipping over. Buicks and Fords and the Chevrolet Bel Air, with its fins slicing away at the evening fog. The Beetle dwarfed in comparison, and so had a man's romantic chances. No amount of punishment Judge Schubert meted out to wayward girls was going to change the equation.

"I heard Jost Dietrich's girl got caught in one of those raids." This was Papa, the barman.

They all turned to Burg to confirm the rumor. Burg nodded. Jost Dietrich was a well-liked cabinet maker who spent four years in a Soviet prisoner of war camp. When he returned, his family was living on potatoes and turnips. They were happy to have their breadwinner back, but there was little demand for fine new cabinets in those lean years. For girls like Jost Dietrich's daughter, the *Amis* held all sorts of promises. Some were actually marrying their soldier boys and even having babies in places like Kansas and Kentucky. But you couldn't tell that to Judge Schubert. To him, they were all *Veronikas*, and the way to save girls like Karl-Heinz's daughter, was to make an example of Jost Dietrich's.

As the evening rolled along, the men bemoaned the lack of any grip they may have had on their own fate. It wasn't so different from their youth, only now it was the occupation and not the Reich that held the cards. "Don't let your priest fool you," Burg was fond of saying. "You can cross yourself all you want, but it's dumb luck if you'll eat tomorrow."

Right before closing, Jost Dietrich burst in and out of breath. With something that resembled too much of a smile on his face, he announced to the assembled regulars, "You're not going to believe this, but Judge Schubert dropped dead this evening."

And then he bought a round of drinks for the five men leaning against Papa's bar, a round he certainly could not afford.

* * * *

No one weeps for the death of a bully. Even at the station the next morning, *Kripos* and *Schupos* alike—from the most senior detective to the newest uniformed—seemed to take the death of Judge Schubert lightly. Only Schmidt looked grim.

The way Jost Dietrich had told it the night before, Schubert's fat face fell right into his soup bowl while he was chewing on a chunk of pumpernickel. At the station, Burg heard the full story.

The chief explained how Schubert's wife was off in Schweinfurt visiting a sister, so Schubert was home alone. When Frau Schubert arrived later expecting her husband in bed, she was surprised to see the lights on in the dining room. She discovered him collapsed at the table with his face in the soup. Jost Dietrich had gotten that part right. Frau Schubert had guessed his heart had finally given out. He'd been to the doctor on and off for palpitations. But it wasn't a heart attack, and he hadn't choked on the pumpernickel.

The chief raised a pointed object up in the air. "This is what killed him."

It was a familiar object to Burg. It looked something like a short sword or a very long knife.

The chief said, "The Mauser 98 bayonet." He looked around at a room filled with men who'd come of age in boots and helmets. "I'm sure you all know how to use one of these…"

Not that we had a chance to use one, Burg thought. Outside of training, there hadn't been much cause. Tanks and machine guns had made bayonets not much more than oversized mess utensils.

"Frau Schubert wasn't completely incorrect about Herr Schubert's heart," the chief said. "It *was* his heart. Only it was this blade that did the damage, not Herr Schubert's fondness for *Schweinshaxen*."

Frau Schubert, the chief explained, had not noticed the bayonet when she discovered her husband slumped over the soup. The assailant had plunged the bayonet into the judge, making a neat slot-shaped hole in his chest. The wound was discovered only when Frau Schubert called for help from her neighbor, the physician Dieter Walter, whose practice in the spas of Bad Kissingen had not called for the treatment of bayonet wounds. Still, during the war Dr. Walter had treated many Wehrmacht soldiers convalescing in Bad Kissingen, so he was familiar with holes in human bodies caused by foreign objects. The chief explained all this in the matter-of-fact manner Burg had grown accustomed to, the way he spoke every morning of traffic accidents, cigarette rackets, and hotel thieves. He put his *Kripos* on the case full time and attached Schmidt to these detectives to assist. The rest of the *Schupos*, including Burg, would stick to routine duties, but with the added task of keeping an ear on the gossip—anything they heard regarding the murder of Judge Schubert they were to report immediately.

Afterward, Burg said to Schmidt, "Looks like you are in for some real detective work. One step closer to the actual job. You'll be a *Kripo* before too long."

Schmidt took a deep breath. "Do you think I'm ready for it?"

"I don't know if hotel raids have prepared either one of us for a promotion. But with Schubert dead, maybe we can all get back to real police work."

Schmidt frowned and turned away. Burg watched him go, and then he remembered Schmidt's somber mood earlier. A joke about the departed was how Burg had often coped with death, but it seemed to him Schmidt wasn't having it, even for a scoundrel like Judge Schubert.

* * * *

Who wouldn't want Schubert dead? By the third day the list of suspects seemed to grow like splitting cancer cells. Numerous GIs had seen their sweethearts sent off to jail. Plenty of those sweethearts had returned to Bad Kissingen after serving Schubert's stiff sentences. How many came home untamed by the humiliation Schubert had inflicted upon them? A girl and a bayonet seemed far-fetched to the Bad Kissingen detectives. Was there an *Ami* boyfriend who would take it upon himself to remove the obstacle between him and his *Fräulein*? A soldier and a bayonet, that seemed more likely.

A nightclub owner who had seen his livelihood extinguished when a Schubert court order shut down his establishment for violating the criminal code concerning indecency, he too was a suspect. From the Bad Kissingen street gossip his remarks were reported as follows: "Lucky for us. Now we can all get back to business."

Jost Dieter was added to the list when a young *Schupo* reported these remarks from the impoverished cabinet maker: "I could build him a lovely coffin, but why waste good wood on the stinking carcass of a *Schweinehund*."

Even the court-appointed social worker fell under suspicion when a woman from her *Kaffeklatch* reported that she had expressed relief rather than sorrow at the passing of the judge.

The whole business was beginning to remind Burg of a novel he had shared with seven prisoners in a bunkhouse in England. They had passed the book around and Burg had read it several times, and it had helped him improve his English. It was about a murder on a train in which every passenger fell under suspicion. Unlike the detective in the novel, Bad Kissingen's small team of *Kripos* began narrowing their list, and although Burg wasn't present at these meetings, Schmidt filled him in.

"They are eliminating the two from our last hotel raid, Sergeant Jones and the Negro," Schmidt said. "The *Amis* claim both shipped out to the training camp in Grafenwöhr the morning their girlfriends were in court."

"Are we just going by their word? You know the *Amis* like to protect their own."

"Nothing but their word. But the chief is going to reach out to the colonel over there. Make a special appeal for cooperation. There are at least two other soldiers on our list still in Bad Kissingen."

"The *Amis* can't hide every GI in Grafenwöhr."

"Neighbors saw one visiting a girlfriend the morning after the murder. She was released from the workhouse two weeks ago. And we still have our eye on that nightclub owner. He lost everything when Schubert shut him down. And he has a lot of friends. Black market types who supplied his club with plenty of American booze. This was in exchange for allowing them to hold shop out of the back of the club. Cigarettes, of course, cans of petrol, tinned food, and frozen beef that went unaccounted from the Daley Barracks mess hall."

"You could make a good *Sauerbraten* with one of their roasts." Burg began to grin and wanted to add "not that I would know myself," but he thought better of it.

"Anyway," Schmidt said," I think it's an *Ami*. You know how they like to collect war relics?"

"There's a brisk business. They pay good dollars and people need the money. Hats and helmets—"

"And any little weapon they can get their hands on."

"Including bayonets."

"Yes, including bayonets." Schmidt stood up to leave.

Burg threw on his coat and stepped outside to begin his foot patrol. Walking along, he daydreamed of his own bayonet, the one he had left in France. When he surrendered, the *Amis* took it, along with his rifle, his wristwatch, and the photo he kept in the pocket of his tunic. But they didn't take his life, and he was grateful for that. Better a year in a camp in wet and miserable England, than an eternity in a grave.

He didn't miss the bayonet, the rifle, the wristwatch. But the photo, he would give a lot to have that back. It was of a girl.

He had been billeted in her village and she had laughed at his clumsy attempts at the French language. He couldn't give her much in terms of favors—he was no well-connected officer—but a tin of horse meat here, a sack of potatoes there, and romance blossomed. Her voice still came to him in his dreams, but her face never appeared, and without the photo he worried his memory would fail him and soon he would have nothing left of it.

He wondered sometimes at her fate. He had seen the photos after the war of French women with heads shorn like sheep and paraded down city streets, shamed for their German lovers. Some had called it "horizontal collaboration."

* * * *

A week went by, and the investigation moved closer to settling on an *Ami*. The GI whose girlfriend had recently returned from the workhouse, he was still under suspicion, but more and more Bad Kissingen's *Kripos* were looking at the other man, a lieutenant by the name of Simon. From street sources they had learned that Simon was a well-known collector of war relics. Iron Crosses and Lugers, and flags hidden under floorboards since 1945. They all came out for Simon, who could pay good money on his officer's salary.

"He's also a notorious womanizer," Schmidt told Burg one afternoon when they were leaving the office. "He keeps two girls in rooms in town. He covers the rent, the bread and butter, the new clothes. And he's known for the occasional tryst with one of the professionals who blow into town every GI payday."

"Seems to me the other *Ami* is your better bet. He sounds devoted. This man, Simon, why would he care if Judge Schubert took away one of his girls? Sounds as if he has at least another to spare."

"He's a hothead. Doesn't want to be told what to do by some old 'Kraut' judge."

"The victor's entitlement."

"Last summer we pulled in one of his girls for violating the prostitution code. They were caught in flagrante delicto in a hotel off Ludwigstrasse. Seems the girl's landlady wasn't having it with the male visitor at all hours of the night, so they took their business to the hotel. The girl got a month in jail."

"An officer's girl?"

"Hard to pull rank when you're pulling up your pants. Anyway, the rumor is this one girl is the lieutenant's favorite, and that he might like her for more than the regular tumble. Now we just need to connect the lieutenant to the bayonet. You'll hear it from the chief tomorrow morning. Keep your ears open on the street, who's been selling war relics."

"Put the bayonet in the lieutenant's hands and you have your case?"

"And *make* our case before the *Amis* get the idea to ship Lieutenant Simon back home."

An hour later Burg found himself back in Eberman's Keller. The regulars were all there and Papa was behind the bar again. Burg tried to imagine one of them selling Lieutenant Simon a bayonet, maybe trading it for cigarettes. A carton of Winstons was like a brick of gold in 1946, and it could still fetch quite a lot in 1952. You could trade cigarettes to feed your family or to buy a favor to get a job. Jost Dietrich could use a job. Burg knew any one of them would be happy with more money, and selling a relic, especially a weapon, could fetch a good price.

He doubted Papa or Karl Heinz would have had a bayonet to trade. They were among the millions of soldiers who surrendered en masse at the end of the war. Any bayonet they may have had was surely confiscated. And would Rudy have clung to his rifle and bayonet as he was carried off the field in the Ukraine, a tourniquet around his thigh to save what was left of his leg? Or Ernst in the Ardennes with his eye torn out? Not likely. But there were other men in other taverns in Bad Kissingen who had served, and any one of them could have kept a bayonet or even a rifle if their circumstances were just right at the end of the war.

Not long after Burg's second beer he got a visit from an *Ami* he had been working, a black man named Sergeant Tower. Tower brought Burg an occasional carton of cigarettes or a bottle of whisky. In exchange, Burg didn't bother if Tower chose to move more merchandise than just a carton or a bottle.

Tower passed Burg a fifth of Wild Turkey and said, "I heard the *Polizei* are coming after a GI over that dead judge."

Burg said, "I'm only a street cop, a *Schupo*. You know more than I do."

"Well, there's something you all don't know about that judge. Or maybe you do but you're just not sharing."

"What's that?"

"He was a big Nazi. You know, we talk over there at Daley, too. Hard to keep a secret around here."

"But if he was a Nazi, he wouldn't be a judge after the war. That's how it worked, didn't it? You *Amis* got rid of all the Nazis."

"We got rid of *most* of them. But you know how it goes with money and connections. A rich dude who ran slave labor through his factory during the war, we'd get rid of him, put him in prison. But with some cash and good anti-red credentials, he might be back running the factory after not too long."

Burg knew all about. "And that rich fellow joined the party in 1933. In '42 a man joined to keep his job, but '33…that meant you were a true believer."

"We tried to clear out all those true believers, but I'll admit, our record is mixed."

"Some of those true believers are back running companies and towns and courts."

"That's because we don't want your country to fall apart…and then fall to the reds."

"And Judge Schubert?" Burg said. "How does he buy his way back?"

"I don't know, but if Uncle Sam wanted him there, he'd be there."

Uncle Sam. Sometimes Burg loved the way the *Amis* talked.

"As far as his killer, my money is on one of *my* kind," Tower said. "We all know how hard Schubert was on the girls who go with colored fellas... now that's an old Nazi if ever there was one. The Nazis didn't like the Jews, and sure as hell didn't like colored people. Yeah, I'd say if any GI killed that judge, he was colored."

Tower threw back the rest of his drink and made an exit.

Burg wanted to say, well, Lieutenant Simon is far from colored. He sat for a minute twirling the remains of his third beer. He was starting to think maybe the Bad Kissingen *Kripos* were too sure about their case. From Schmidt's description, it sounded as if they were all but certain on the *Ami* angle. And they were riding a train they couldn't stop, with Lieutenant Simon as their ultimate *Endstation*.

Schubert as a Nazi, that wasn't a surprise. The way the man had gone about cleaning up Bad Kissingen of *Veronikas*, it was all too familiar. Burg remembered the clean-up not so long ago, only it was Jews and *Untermenschen* back then. Schubert's severity in court with those wild girls, it was no different than the zealotry Burg had seen in the '30s, when young men in brown shirts smashed windows, or kicked to the ground grandfathers with stars stitched to their chests.

The more Burg thought about it, the more he came to believe the Bad Kissingen *Kripos* were wrong. The thing to do was not to narrow the list of suspects, but to expand it. Should he tell this to Schmidt? Maybe Schmidt would pass this suggestion on to the men running the case. Or should he keep it to himself, maybe tell the chief on his own? It would be a step toward his own place at the table. In short time he could leave the ranks of *Schupos*, become a *Kripo* himself. *Kriminalkommisar* Hans Burg—it sounded pretty good. He thought he could do the job as well as any of the men already there, and certainly better than Schmidt. All he needed was the ambition.

The bayonet was still the key. If it couldn't be placed in Lieutenant Simon's hands, then who else? Maybe an *Ami* veteran, not a young conscript out to find a girl and happy he wasn't in Korea, but a bit older, someone who had seen action here, freezing in Bastogne or crossing the Rhine. He makes the judge pay for the death of a comrade. Or even a Wehrmacht veteran, someone like him. The judge must pay for leading Germany down a sewer hole, for all the pointless deaths on the Eastern Front. Something like that. These possibilities, and more, Burg ran through his head like a chess match as he took a fourth beer. He sat alone at the table, the murmur of voices at the bar the only distraction. One particular possibility was starting to scratch at him like a rash. Perhaps, he thought, when all the bright *Kripos* were looking at the war relic, at the bayonet, they were looking at the wrong war.

* * * *

He dreamed that night of his French girl. It was the same as always. Her voice speaking to him in the dark, from around the corner, from the other room. In the morning, he cleared the bottle of Wild Turkey into the cupboard, sat for his breakfast, and began to consider again the bayonet.

In the first war the bayonet was a much more useful weapon. If you made it to the enemy's trench and you met him up close, and if you had already fired your rifle, then you had to rely on the bayonet to take his life—and to save your own. Burg had heard this from his father. Burg had also learned from his father that the rifle Burg carried into Poland in 1939 wasn't much different from the rifle his father had carried in 1917. The Karabiner 98 had been around since 1898, only to evolve into several iterations. His father killed Frenchmen with the Karabiner 98A, and Burg fought his own war with the Karabiner 98K. It was something the press in 1939 didn't mention as the Wehrmacht roared its way east—that the rank-and-file infantry soldier was carrying a rifle not much different from his father's some twenty years before. The propaganda machine may have swooned at the squadrons of tanks blitzing into Poland, but they forgot to mention the thousands of horses drawing wagons loaded with supplies. Not all war-making tools were as modern and impressive as the mighty German panzers, and one of these was the rifle of the lowly private Hans Burg. What all this meant, Burg determined as he poured bitter coffee into himself, was that the bayonet for his father's rifle was essentially the same as the one issued to him on his own first campaign.

In the office that morning, he asked Schmidt about the lead on the bayonet.

Schmidt said, "Nothing much to find. Whoever killed Schubert scratched off the serial number. If Lieutenant Simon killed the judge, then he tried to make sure we couldn't trace who might have sold it to him. Not that we even could. We might have been able to determine place and date of manufacture, but nothing after that. You remember how it was at the end."

"Chaos. A quartermaster's hell. Equipment lost, abandoned, stolen."

"Exactly. But someone in Bad Kissingen sold a bayonet to Simon. That's our angle. Find the man who sold the bayonet, and we've got our case."

"So, it's still Lieutenant Simon? And the other *Ami*? The one with the girl just out of the workhouse?"

"He's in the American hospital in Würzburg. Thrown out of a jeep during training. Bad news for him, good news for us. If he's our killer, the *Amis* can't ship him back to the States in his condition. But I'm putting my money on Simon."

"Simon. That's a Jewish name, isn't it?"

Schmidt seemed to wince. "I hadn't thought of that."

It had been something to not think about for years, Burg wanted to say, but he kept the thought to himself. There was a time when you might wonder if your neighbor was a Jew, someone who looked and dressed like you but went to synagogue on Saturdays. But that time had passed. Burg was a teenager then, and Schmidt only a child. Now Germany had no synagogues and was empty of Jews, or nearly so.

Burg exited the station to make his usual patrol, the *Schupo* work he could see Schmidt leaving soon. He walked down Maxstrasse and turned south into the town center. *Hausfraus* on bicycles carried bread and vegetables in their baskets. Gray-headed men smoked on benches in the central square, Marktplatz, where the city hall rose up with an onion-shaped tower. Which of these men, Burg wondered, carried a Mauser 98 bayonet thirty-five years ago? Further on he entered the spa district. The gardens had recovered since the war, and now the patients had returned. Some people had money again and could afford a *Kur*, massages and mud baths and curious diets. He watched them and considered their renewed prosperity—the black market, perhaps. He circled back on his regular route. In his uniform he was a public presence, to say law and order and normalcy had returned. As he headed for Marienplatz, where the steeple of the Herz Jesu Kirche towered over the largest fountain in town, he crossed in front of the Bäckarei Kraus. He stopped and turned. Burg was not only acquainted with the baker Herr Kraus, but also with his strudel, which had the reputation as the best in Bad Kissingen.

In the shop he said his pleasantries, ordered a portion of the strudel and ate it there at a café table. He watched Herr Kraus do his work, which didn't seem so bad, although he still would hate the idea of working in the night to meet the demands of patrons coming through the door in the early morning. Herr Kraus moved an empty tray from the display case, returning with another, fresh and full. Kraus, Burg thought, was too young for the first war. If he had sold a bayonet to Lieutenant Simon, or had killed Schubert himself, it would have been with one from the second war. But Burg recalled that Kraus had not served in the initial call up, only much later as they conscripted men in their thirties and forties. Maybe he was somewhere far away from the action, cooking or baking bread to feed the war machine.

And then he watched Frau Kraus enter from the back. The shop was empty except for Burg, and the couple must have forgotten he was there, because they spoke as if in private, with an affection reserved for private. Frau Kraus said *"Liebling"* and Herr Kraus returned the endearment. To be their age and settled and to still…well, it surprised Burg. Then Frau Kraus noticed him. She said hello and then returned into the back, clearly embarrassed by her affectionate talk. Now Burg remembered the rumor from years ago of how their families had disapproved, and Burg wondered if that had made their match all the more enduring.

When Burg finished his patrol, he changed out of his uniform and made his way to Ebermans. There was talk again around the bar about Jost Dietrich. His daughter was off with a new GI, and this one was serious.

Papa said, "Maybe this fellow will last. With Schubert dead, she won't be thrown into the jail. They will have time for love to grow."

There was a murmur of snickers.

"But haven't you heard?" Karl-Heinz said. "This one is a Negro."

Their mirth evaporated.

"Well, that complicates the matter." This was Papa again.

"And I've heard the man wants to marry her," Karl-Heinz said.

"The *Amis* won't allow it. They don't like mixed marriages, and the men have to get permission from their commander to marry."

"From the colonel?"

"Yes. And if he doesn't like the match, he will say no. Even ship the Negro soldier out, maybe to Korea, far away from his sweetheart."

Rudy turned to Burg and said, "Hans, what do you think?" Burg was a cop, and they expected him to know such things.

Burg took a long pull on his beer and said, "I have no idea."

At home that night Burg couldn't sleep. Even the remains of the Wild Turkey couldn't stop his mind from calculating.

What Karl-Heinz had said about Jost Dietrich's daughter marrying the Negro soldier set off another formula in Burg's mind, one that he now connected to a memory of a mixed marriage and the trouble that came with it.

When half the night was lost and he had at last given up on sleep, Burg threw on his coat and went for a walk. A light rain came on, but he was wearing his felt hat, so the damp wasn't a bother. He tried to tell himself this was only a random stroll, an insomniac's promenade, but he knew that wasn't true. He had a destination, definite and unforgiving. He turned past the Herz Jesu Kirche, past the dormant fountain now only trembling with rain drops, and not long after found himself where he had been only a half-day before, at the door of the Bäkerei Kraus.

The baker was up, he knew, but in the back where the oven stood, so he knocked hard. Herr Kraus appeared with a rolling pin in his hand, a weapon against intruders. When he saw that it was Burg the policeman, he laid down the rolling pin and came to unlock the door.

"Herr Burg," Kraus said, "what brings you around in the middle of the night? Is there some trouble?" Kraus looked past Burg, up and down the street, for a car or some flashing lights.

"No," Burg said, "only some questions…about an investigation."

"At this hour? Seems a strange time to conduct an investigation."

"I know, I'm sorry. I couldn't sleep and thought for sure you would be up. I hope you don't mind. It will save a half-hour of your time in the morning."

Kraus opened the door to let Burg in.

Burg said, "If you don't mind, it's Frau Kraus I'd like to speak with."

The baker looked puzzled. But then he shrugged his shoulders and left to fetch his wife. When she appeared, Herr Kraus said, "I'll be in the back," and then he returned to his oven.

Frau Kraus motioned to a small café table with the chairs turned up. She set the chairs on their legs and the two of them sat. In the dim light Burg began to imagine this was how an interrogation went, if he were a detective, a *Kripo*.

"Have you been following the murder of Judge Schubert in the papers?"

"Of course. Haven't we all?"

"Then you know how he was killed?"

"Stabbed, that's what the papers say."

"That's right."

Burg paused for too long, and then Frau Kraus said, "You want to ask me about Herr Schubert? Frau Schubert buys their bread from us."

"Actually…I want to ask about your father."

"My father?"

"Yes."

"I see."

Burg pulled off his hat and held it in his lap. "My father served with your father in the first war."

"Oh…I didn't recall. My father didn't talk much about the war. I'm sorry, Herr Burg, but what does this have to do with—"

"He was a hero, your father. Iron Cross 1st Class. My father told me."

"Yes…well, that was a long time ago." She looked up at the clock, at the late hour. "I think we are all tired of wars now."

"It was a shame what happened to him."

Frau Kraus blinked her eyes slowly, holding them closed for a long moment. "It's as if it never happened. No one talks about it. They all want to forget. Today is today and yesterday is in the past."

"Still, you haven't forgotten…I thought maybe I had, but I haven't either." Burg cleared his throat. "They pulled him out of his office and beat him in the street. Your mother was crying over him as he lay there bleeding. They ransacked his office. I saw one of them come out with his Iron Cross. He shoved it in your father's face and then slapped him hard and called him a thief, as if your father had stolen the Iron Cross."

"I wasn't there. My mother told me some of what happened, but she saved me from the worst details."

"Oh…" Burg shifted in his seat. He wanted to bite back what he'd said. "Your mother… I remember your mother."

"She was a fool to listen to him. They should have emigrated. One of my uncles did, and plenty of others. At least half of us. But Papa wouldn't leave. He said the insanity would pass. Instead of new lives in the States, or in South America, he stayed until it was too late."

Burg stared down at his hat and worked the brim with his fingers. "I remember…I remember your wedding. I was a kid, but I remember. You had red hair back then."

"A long time ago." Frau Schubert pulled at a strand by her ear. "It's faded, I'm afraid."

"Your father invited my family. I was a kid, still in short pants."

A picture passed through Burg's head, vibrant as a hand-colored photograph. The bride's red hair against a white dress, both hands gripping a bundle of long green stems, the stems carrying blossoms of blue irises.

"Then you know what they said?"

"Scandal…from the ladies in my mother's *Kaffeklatch*. I overheard it and went to the dictionary to look it up."

"'Good Catholic Boy Marries Jew Girl.' It might as well have been a headline in the *Völkischer Beobachter*. You know, there were over three-hundred of us. We owned hotels, restaurants. Doctors and nurses in the spas. Then they forbade us from sharing the baths. Then the children couldn't go to school together. In '38 they burned the synagogue down and began sending the men away. That was the end of it…only the Jew girl who married the good Catholic boy remained… My husband, he says they liked his strudel too much to send me away."

"Schubert was eating your husband's pumpernickel when he died."

"He loved that pumpernickel. His wife was away, so I stopped at his house and told him she had called asking for a fresh order for his dinner. He let me right in. A Jew in his house. I thought maybe he'd forgotten…forgotten how he'd thrown my father into the streets, calling him a thief." She shook her head.

There was a long silence before Burg said, "I thought maybe you had sold your father's bayonet to an *Ami* named Simon. He is also a Jew." Knowing it wasn't true, hoping she would say *yes, that's right*.

"You're clever, Herr Burg. The papers didn't say it was a bayonet. Only that Herr Schubert had been stabbed. My father defended this country with that blade, and I defended his honor."

Burg cleared his throat. "And the Iron Cross?"

"I found it in Schubert's desk drawer. It was lying there next to his bible. I took it and slipped out of the house. I have it upstairs in my nightstand… You know, my father loved Germany. He didn't even go to synagogue. I think Germany was his temple. He listened to Beethoven, read Schiller…"

"With the way Schubert was carrying on, locking up girls, embarrassing their families, aggravating the *Amis* to no end…"

"Everybody wanted him dead."

"A good cover. Almost as good as a solid alibi."

They sat for a long moment, and then Herr Kraus popped his head through the doorway. "Everything okay?"

"Everything is fine my dear. Go back to your work."

Herr Kraus disappeared behind the door. Burg stood up and lifted his hat to his head.

"I'm going home now. In the morning I'll come for you. That will give you time to explain to Herr Kraus."

"Thank you for that."

When Burg stepped back onto the street she was still sitting there at the little table, her eyes closed, as if asleep or in meditation. He walked home in the rain and the dark, and even before he arrived at his place to throw himself into bed, he had already made up his mind.

In the morning the chief would call in all the *Schupos* and *Kripos* to report they had waited too long. Lieutenant Simon had flown away to America and now their case was dead. But the *Schupo* Schmidt had done good work, and soon he would see a promotion. But Burg was thinking of his French girl, whose face he could no longer see…and of Frau Kraus…and of how Schubert, in all his efforts to clean up Germany, could not destroy every match of sweethearts. It would take the last Jew in Bad Kissingen to put an end to Schubert and his chaos. Burg would say nothing. He would not help Schubert in his work splitting up lovers.

He would wonder what Frau Kraus would say to him the next time he stopped in for a portion of the best strudel in Bad Kissingen. Would she ask him why he did not return in the morning to take her away? And would she put a light hand on her husband's shoulder as he changed a tray in the display case, a lover's hand, a soft and secret touch of affection?

Matthew Wilson is a teacher from Portland, Oregon. He lived for three years in Bad Kissingen, Germany, the setting of "The Hotel Raids." His Hans Burg stories have previously appeared in *Ellery Queen's Mystery Magazine* and *Alfred Hitchcock's Mystery Magazine*. He also writes mystery stories set in contemporary times, one of which, "Thank You For Your Service," was selected for *The Best American Mystery and Suspense 2022*.

VELDA GETS SKINNED

RON MILLER

As was all too usual, I was loafing around my apartment wondering where my next cheeseburger was coming from. Cases—paying cases—had been few and far between…also as usual. As tough as things were, I still wouldn't trade where I was now for even one day back in the Follies because, frankly, even starving to death was better than stripping every evening for a bunch of bug-eyed winos at Slotnik's Follies. I might waste away to nothing, but at least I would do so decently dressed.

I was chewing on my fingernails, which were about the only thing I had in the place to eat, when the phone rang. This really surprised me since I'd supposed the phone company had shut off my service days ago. I answered it before they could realize their mistake.

"Bellinghausen Superior Detective Agency," I said in my most professional-sounding voice. "How may I direct your call?"

"This is Rollo Dermis," came a rather distinguished-sounding reply. "I would like to speak to Miss Bellinghausen if she is free."

"Please hold the line. I will see if she has a moment."

I put my hand over the receiver and counted to ten.

"This is Miss Bellinghausen."

"This is Rollo Dermis. I'm president of the Sunnybuns Naturist Society. Your name came highly recommended by one of our members, Miss Shakewell."

He must have meant Fizzy Shakewell, one of the classier strippers at the Follies. What she was doing belonging to any kind of society eluded me. She had even been rejected by the Brownies.

"We need a detective," the voice continued, "one whose discretion we can rely upon."

"Discretion is my middle name," I replied, though it really wasn't.

"Excellent! The address is 1407 Cowpasture Lane, Saltlick."

"I know where that is." It was a half-pint village a few miles up the Hudson. There had been a swell axe murder there last year and I had read all about it. "I can be there in a couple of hours."

"We are about a mile east of town. I will explain everything when you get here. I am reluctant to go into any further details over the telephone. I am sure you understand?"

"Of course," I lied. "I'm on my way now."

I hung up the phone, thinking: *Gee! A naturist society! I* love *nature!*

* * * *

I talked Joe out of his Buick and fifty-eight minutes later I was outside the city tooling through the countryside looking for Cowpasture Road when I spotted a small, neatly painted sign: *Sunnybuns Naturist Society—1 mile.* Exactly one mile later, another sign directed me onto a narrow, graveled side road, flanked on both sides by rail fences. Topped with barbed wire, for Pete's sake.

I was wondering what kind of bird-watchers would need a detective when I came to a gate. It was festooned with signs warning me that beyond was *PRIVATE PROPERTY*, that there was to be *NO TRESPASSING!* and to *KEEP OUT!*

There was a little box atop a pole just about at window level, kind of like one of the speakers at a drive-in movie. A tinny voice came from it.

"Who is it?"

"Velda Bellinghausen, to see Mr. Dermis."

The voice said to please come in as I heard a click, and the gate swung open.

Pretty shy for a bunch of bird watchers, I thought. Then, as I drove up the lane beyond the gate, I began to have second thoughts about that.

There were tidy lawns to either side of the drive and there was a man pushing a lawn mower. He waved to me and kept on working, which was all well and good and except for the fact that he was stark naked seemed perfectly normal for life out in the sticks, I suppose.

A hundred feet further along there were half a dozen men and women playing volleyball. They were all stark naked, too, and seemed to be having a pretty good time.

Apparently, bird watchers weren't as shy as I'd thought they'd be.

The office was a tidy little log place painted white, with a sign over the door that said *Sunnybuns Naturist Society—Office* so I knew I had gotten where I was supposed to go.

I don't know why I was particularly surprised to find a receptionist—a small, slim brunette with a figure that would have made her a headliner at the Follies—busily typing and totally nude. She looked up when I came in. She took her glasses off, making her about one half of one percent nuder than before, and smiled at me.

"You must be Miss Bellinghausen! Mr. Dermis is expecting you! You can go right in," she said, gesturing toward a closed door behind her.

I began to wonder if I had perhaps erred in some way.

I went through the door and decided that I *had* erred.

There was a man sitting behind a busy-looking desk. He was kind of portly, had thinning gray hair and pince-nez glasses balanced on his nose, if pince-nez is the word I mean. He looked like the vice president of a small but prosperous savings and loan except for being completely naked, of course. I'd never taken out a loan—let alone ever having had enough money to have a bank account—but I was pretty sure that vice presidents of savings and loans usually wore clothes. At least when they expected company, at any rate.

"Miss Bellinghausen!" he said, bursting into a smile and starting to get to his feet.

"Please don't get up on my account," I said.

"It's really good of you to come on such short notice and with such little explanation. You will soon see why I had to be discreet."

"I can imagine that discretion *is* pretty important around here."

* * * *

The next five minutes were enlightening. You might not know this, but naturism doesn't have anything at all to do with bird-watching or collecting flowers. Sunnybuns Naturist Society was really a nudist colony, which was a surprise to me. I mean, I suppose that being naked *is* perfectly natural…after all, we're born that way and, well, we all know what I did at the Follies…but it seemed to me that it was kind of dishonest to not call the place what it was. Kind of embarrassing, too, if you don't expect it.

Anyway, while these thoughts were running through my mind, Mr. Dermis had been explaining his problem to me. I figured I hadn't missed too much since he was apparently only just then getting around to the point. So I nodded like I'd been listening to every word all along.

"Terrible crimes are being committed here at Sunnybuns," he was saying.

"I imagine it's not pickpocketing."

"You see, it's strictly against the society's rules for its members to wear any clothing while on the property or outside their cabins. This includes even watches and jewelry. Since the grounds are closed to strangers, the members have no qualms about leaving such things lying about. But recently, items, valuable items, have been disappearing from cabins while their occupants are away."

"I suppose a stranger around here would kind of stand out."

"Of course. Yet there's no possibility of suspecting one of our members."

"Sure. Of course not."

"So you see our difficulty? If there is in fact a thief among us, we must ferret them out…and as discreetly as possible, of course."

"Are there any employees? I mean other than your receptionist and yourself?"

"Well, yes…yes, there are two. A sort of gardener-handyman and his wife. Keeps the place tidy and makes sure everything is running smoothly. Changes the light bulbs, fixes the iceboxes, runs into town for supplies, that sort of thing, you know. His wife is our cook."

I just stared.

"Well, all right," Dermis squirmed, wringing his hands as though they were kitchen sponges, "maybe I *have* had my doubts, but…"

"But?"

"Well…while the club pays the Skinners—Lester and Wanda Skinner—a fair wage it is, I am afraid, a modest one. However, they're provided a cabin and meals as well as free use of the club vehicle."

"Would you have any reason to think they're thieves?"

"Well, no…not exactly. I did notice recently, about the same time the robberies began, that Mr. Skinner bought a car. Admittedly, it was an older model and a pretty well-used one at that, but still, it made me wonder."

"I see your point."

"So I'm hoping that you might look around—discreetly of course!" he added hastily.

"Discretion is my middle name," I replied, though it isn't. "I'd be glad to take a look around and see what I can turn up."

I turned to go when Mr. Dermis cried out. "Oh! Miss Bellinghausen! You can't go out like *that*!"

"Pardon?"

"Our *rules*! They are *very* strict!"

* * * *

Five minutes later found me in a locker room, peeling myself like a banana. *The things*, I thought, *I won't do to pay the rent*. Well, I'd spent five years in the Follies doing pretty much the same thing as I was doing right now, so I didn't know what I was kicking about.

Still…it *did* seem different somehow.

It seemed even more so when I stepped outside. By then, it was early afternoon, and the place was pretty busy. There were people at the swimming pool and people doing calisthenics and people playing tennis and badminton and volleyball and croquet and people sitting around little circular tables under umbrellas playing cards or chess and people just lounging in the sun. There were people old enough to be my grandparents and there were teenagers and little kids just barely able to crawl around. And every last one of them was as naked as I was.

Aside from being naked, there was one other quality I noticed after a few moments. Everyone looked as healthy as an Ovaltine ad. The old people looked as though they did a hundred push-ups before breakfast and the toddlers looked like they chewed on three-penny nails instead of pacifiers. I suddenly felt self-consciously skinny, pale and underfed.

I walked around a little, just to get the lay of the place, and after a few minutes I realized what was so uncanny about the whole thing. When I shed my feathers at the Follies, which I did every evening and two times on weekends with matinees, I had every eye in the place glued to me. But this was different and what made it so disconcerting, if disconcerting is the word I want, was that no one seemed to care. Not one single person did more than glance at me before going back to their ball game or book or knitting or whatever they were doing.

Weirdly enough, the effect was that, for the first time in my life, I felt self-conscious about not having any clothes on. I didn't like that very much.

"Say, Velda!"

I recognized that voice before I even turned around to see Fizzy Shakewell running up the path toward me. She was a platinum blonde nearly as tall as I am, but where I am built more along the lines of Suzy Parker, Fizzy had been cast from the Jayne Mansfield mold. *Vogue* vs. *Rogue* if you get my drift.

She pulled up to a stop next to me, though most of her body kept moving.

"Mr. Dermis told me that you'd taken the case," she said. "Sorry I wasn't here when you arrived. The book club was still meeting."

I wanted to say, "Book?" since I had never known Fizzy to read anything more complicated than a comic book, but I liked her, so I just smiled and replied, "That's okay. I knew I'd be running into you eventually. Thanks for the tip. I really needed the job."

"What're friends for anyway, right, Velda?"

"Sure thing, Fizzy. Say, is there a motel in town and maybe a shop where I can get a few things? I think this is going to take a couple of days and I didn't think to bring along an overnight bag."

"Don't worry about any of that. I fixed it up with Mr. Dermis for you to have one of the empty cabins. It's right over there by the duck pond. I hope you like ducks. I think they're funny. You don't need no clothes here and there's clean towels and soap in the cabin and I got an extra toothbrush you can have."

I always sleep in the raw anyway so that seemed to take care of that, so I asked her about the robberies.

"Happened to me just yesterday, can you believe it! I had all my things sitting on top of the dresser like always and the next morning everything was gone!"

"Things like what things?"

"My wristwatch and a necklace and a couple of rings. They weren't worth a whole lot, except maybe the watch, but they was all presents from Slotnik so they had great sentimental value."

I could just imagine. *Anything* from that penny-pinching Slotnik would be a rarity. I never even got the time of day from Slotnik let alone a watch. Just went to show how big a star Fizzy had become.

"Can I see your place? I'd like to look around a little."

"Sure! I ain't never seen a detective detect before!"

Her cabin was exactly like a couple of dozen others scattered around the property. A simple frame place, about twenty by twenty, with a bathroom, bedroom, and combination living room, dining room and kitchen. Fizzy pointed out the scene of the crime to me.

"The dresser always under the window?"

"Sure."

"Was the window open last night?"

"Why, yes it was!"

"Was anything else taken?"

"No, now that you mention it. In fact, my purse was right there, too. It had all my money in it, so it was the first thing I checked when I saw that my jewelry was gone. But it was okay. Nothing had been touched."

"I'd like to look around some more, maybe ask some questions. You think the other members would be all right with that?"

"Oh, sure! I told everyone you were coming. The whole gang is looking forward to meeting you!"

* * * *

Pretty much everyone had the same story, as it turned out. "I leave my valuables out all the time," was the typical reply to my first question, "and never had anything stolen." And when I asked about windows, the answer was either "I keep them open all the time" or "I keep them shut but never locked. No one ever locks anything around here."

It didn't take too long for me to see a glimmering of some sort of pattern. The members who kept their windows shut never had anything taken, but if a window happened to be open, it was an invitation to the thief. Not once did I hear of the thief ever opening a window, even if it had been unlocked. And he never searched through clothing or drawers. He took only what was out in the open, clearly visible to anyone looking from the outside. It was a pattern all right but, like a Chinese menu, it looked pretty but didn't mean a thing to me.

But what really beat me was this: Where in the world do you hide loot in a nudist colony?

By the time I'd spoken to a couple of dozen people, it was growing dark, so I decided to put off any further investigation until the following morning.

I had dinner with Fizzy and Mr. Dermis in the crowded dining hall, which was probably the most disconcerting experience of my life. But the food was great.

Dinner was served buffet-style, with platters and bowls of food spread down the length of a large table at one end of the room. Hovering over this was a small, portly woman who probably would have reminded me of Mrs. Santa Claus under any other circumstances.

As I dug into some pretty good chow, I asked Mr. Dermis if the woman by the buffet was Mrs. Skinner. He said, yes, that was she.

"Her husband around anywhere?"

"Probably out at the well. We've had a few problems with the pump today."

He told me where that was and after a little chit chat about this and that, I left Fizzy and Dermis and went off to look for Lester Skinner.

Finding the pump house was easy and as I got closer to it, I could hear a lot of banging, sounding just like when I have to bang on my radiator in the winter to get Mr. Saperstein to turn on the heat.

The pump house was little more than a shed and the door was hanging open. As I came around it, I saw in the dark interior what at first looked like two cantaloupes, but which just proved to be Mr. Skinner as he turned at the sound of my approach.

He was a small man, nearly as wide as he was tall, whose head barely came to my collarbone. He resembled Mickey Rooney if Mickey Rooney were thirty years older and naked.

"Hello," he said, wiping his greasy palms on his hairy thighs and then extending one to me. "New here, aren't you?"

I took his paw gingerly between my fingers and said, yes, this was my first day.

"Well, take my advice and get yourself some good bug repellent. The mosquitoes here'll drain you dry given half a chance. Better get some Coppertone, too, if you ain't got any already. Pale girl like you'll burn to a crisp in no time."

"I'll do that, thanks."

"That your car?" I asked, pointing to the heap parked behind the pump house. "It's the only one not in the lot out front."

"Sure is! Nice job ain't she?" He walked around the shed and ran his hand over a fender. "Got her for a steal, I did."

I wondered if truer words had ever been spoken.

* * * *

I was pretty exhausted by the time I got back to my cabin, but before I fell into bed, I thought I'd try an experiment. I had a little chain with a pewter mascot on it that Chip had won for me at Coney Island. I put it on top of the dresser and opened the window over it, just to see what might happen. Then I turned out the lights, crawled between the cool sheets and was soon dreaming that I was at my high school prom with no clothes on.

The next morning, the chain was gone.

I found that the little kitchen in my cabin had been kindly stocked with food, so I made myself a scrambled egg and toast and a mug of black coffee. I decided that frying some bacon might be a little too dangerous.

It was a beautiful, sunny day and even though I was out and about at an hour that was pretty early for me, there were already dozens of nudists running around the place, doing all of those strenuous things that seem to make them so happy. I found myself a deck chair near the volleyball court and stretched out in it with a Coke I'd found in my icebox.

Instead of batting a ball back and forth, a dozen men and women were holding hands and prancing around in a circle, which looked silly to me, but they seemed happy, I guess, so I leaned back into my chair and sipped my soft drink.

The sun was warm and there was a light breeze that felt like a sheet of cool silk rippling over my body, and I decided that I could probably get used to this sort of thing pretty quickly. Especially if those Morris dancers didn't show up every day.

I wondered what my old pal Chip would think if he could see me now. Probably have an embolism.

All of this was pretty amusing, but I thought I'd at least better make a show of earning my fee. Besides, I wanted to see more of the camp, which kind of interested me since I'm not really much of an outdoor girl as you have probably figured out.

The whole camp, I learned, had once been a farm owned by some relative or another of Mr. Dermis. So there were lots of open fields as well as a little woods with a path snaking through it and a pretty large pond with canoes. Wandering around and hoping I was looking more casual than I felt, I ran across most of the members I hadn't met the day before. I didn't learn any more than I had already, which was what I expected. Everyone had the same story, more or less. What kind of surprised me, though, was how nice everyone was. I think I kind of expected a lot of fanatics, like vegetarians or those people who think the earth is flat, but they were all so pleasant that it wasn't long before I forgot that we were all of us stark naked.

It was still an hour or so before noon so I thought I might wander over to the dining hall on the off chance of catching Mrs. Skinner alone.

The place was, as I'd hoped, empty. Except for the chubby little lady who was bustling around the room dropping buds into the glass flower vase that sat in the middle of every table.

"Good morning!" she said cheerfully. "You're lucky! I still have plenty of good, hot coffee left over from breakfast!"

"Just what I need," I replied as I made my way to a table.

"My goodness," she said as she came up to me with a big silver coffee pot in one hand and a big mug in the other. She was so small I was surprised to not see her tip over onto her face. "My goodness, but you're certainly a tall girl!"

Sitting down, I discovered that I still had a couple of inches on her.

"I guess what all my friends have been telling me is true."

"You're the new member here, aren't you?" she asked as she poured my coffee.

"Just got in yesterday."

"You'll like Sunnybuns!"

"It's very nice but it does take a little getting used to."

"Just give it a few days, it'll all soon seem perfectly natural!"

"I'm sure." I sucked on my coffee, which was very good. "Have you and

Mr. Skinner been here long?"

"Oh, my goodness, yes, indeed! Almost from the very day Sunnybuns opened!"

She really talked like that, with every sentence ending in a ! except for the ones that ended with a ?.

"You must really like it."

"Oh, my, yes! We live here, you know, year-round! Someone has to watch over things during the off season! Mr. Skinner finds plenty of work to do at the farms around here!"

"He must do pretty well. Your husband showed me your new car yesterday."

"Isn't it a dandy? We came into a little extra money recently and we've never had a proper automobile of our own!"

Extra money, eh?

After chatting a little more about this, that, and the other I went back out to the pool. Now all of the tanned bodies doing all sorts of attractive athletic things around me were no longer a distraction. Instead, I wondered about Mr. and Mrs. Skinner. I really didn't want to suspect them of something as petty as robbery. They were just too nice. They reminded me of Mr. and Mrs. Saperstein back home. He always had a cheerful word for me when he came up to fix my plumbing and she always had some freshly baked cookies for me. Perhaps it was the Skinner's resemblance to Santa and Mrs. Claus, though Mr. Skinner didn't have a beard, and both were naked. But still...they seemed like such *nice* people.

But then again, some of the worst ax murderers I have ever known looked like choir boys, so who can tell?

"Miss Bellinghausen?"

I opened my eyes and raised my sunglasses to find Mr. Skinner standing beside my deck chair, looking like a boiled potato. He was wringing his hands like a fretful schoolgirl.

"Yeah?"

"I know who you are, Miss Bellinghausen. *What* you are, I mean."

I just raised my eyebrows and frowned in what I thought would be a quizzical expression.

"I was watering the hellebores under the window of Mr. Dermis's office and I heard him talking."

"And...?"

"And, well, he was talking about *you*, Miss Bellinghausen. About... about you being a detective and all."

He paused, apparently waiting for me to say something. I didn't and after a minute he gave up.

"I—I done it, Miss Bellinghausen. It was me done it."

"You mean you...?"

"With my little Kodak. I done it."

"What are you talking about?"

"I took the pictures, Miss Bellinghausen. I know I shouldn't have done it, I know that now. It was wrong, Miss Bellinghausen, really wrong and I'm sorry."

"What pictures? What the hell are you talking about?"

"The pictures for the magazine, Miss Bellinghausen. *Suntan Month-ly*. They paid me and the missus fifty dollars for pictures of Sunnybuns. I couldn't help it. We needed a car bad."

What in the world? I thought. I looked again at the chubby little man, practically dissolving before my eyes in a frenzy of sheer guilt and anxiety. What did I care about pictures?

"Look," I said, "I don't really care about you and your camera. I have no idea what you heard Mr. Dermis say, but I'm not here because of any pictures. You can take all the pictures around here you want, for all the difference it makes to me."

"Really?"

"Really," I said as I watched him congeal with relief. "Bring your camera around later and I'll show you."

* * * *

Well, that put me back on square one.

I leaned back in the lounge chair and closed my eyes again, but all of my deep thoughts were interrupted by a chirpy voice saying, "Hiya, Velda!"

It was Fizzy, of course. I opened my eyes, squinted and replied, "Hello, Fizzy."

Taking this as an invitation, she plopped down onto the empty chair next to mine.

"I hear that you've been talking to pretty much everyone in the camp."

"I guess so."

"Any ideas yet?"

"Not a one. Except for the fact that they're all naked, they seem like perfectly regular people to me. Besides, pretty much everyone seems to have had something stolen at one time or another. And everyone here seems to be pretty well off. I mean, what would be the point of stealing anything? And if someone did, why trinkets and doodads when purses and wallets would be such easy pickings?"

"Well, if anyone can figure this out, you will!"

"I appreciate your confidence."

"Saw you talking to Mr. Skinner as I was coming across the lawn."

"Yeah. He seems like a pretty nice old duffer."

"You didn't suspect *him*, did you?"

"No, of course not," I lied. "He was just telling me about his hobby."

"I didn't know that Mr. Skinner had a hobby."

I pulled my sunglasses down my nose and looked over them at Fizzy. Jesus. She has more curves than a bowl of spaghetti. As usual, she made me feel like a broomstick with a pair of gumdrops stuck to it. If anything would attract a Kodak like a brand-new dime attracts Rockefeller, it would be Fizzy. Why Skinner would have wasted film on anyone else in the camp escaped me.

"You ever see *Suntan Monthly?*" I asked.

"No…but I've heard of it."

"You might want to take a look at the next issue."

* * * *

I lounged around for maybe an hour after that, nursing this thought and the other, when I finally became conscious of something that had been nagging at the back of my mind. There was a big tree on the far side of the playing field, maybe a couple of hundred feet away from where I sat. It was right on the property line, a tall, barbed wire-topped fence separating it from the road that lay about ten or fifteen feet below. What had been bothering me was something glinting in the sunlight somewhere in the tree's upper branches. Whenever the breeze wafted through, it would twinkle so I wondered what it could be.

Fortunately, there were some *real* birdwatchers among the nudists. A nice-looking lady was sitting on a bench by the path maybe twenty feet away from me. She would have probably jolted the cucumber sandwiches out of her bridge club back home were they to see her now. She had a little book in her lap and a pair of binoculars glued to her eyes. I reluctantly hauled myself out of my chair and strolled over to her.

"Mind if I take a look through those?" I asked. "There's something funny in that tree over there."

She said, sure, anything for a fellow ornithologist, which I took for a compliment since she seemed like a decent old bird.

I put the glasses to my eyes and screwed the focus up and down until the distant tree came in sharp and clear. I slowly scanned around that part where I'd thought I'd seen the twinkle and spotted it almost right away. There was a bundle of twigs stuck to one of the branches and tangled up in it was a bunch of stuff that sparkled in the sunlight. Right next to the pile of junk was a funny-looking black and white bird.

"What's that funny-looking bird?" I asked the old lady.

She took the glasses from me, took a look and said, "That's a magpie, honey."

"What the hell is a magpie?"

"It is a common bird in the same family as the jay and crow. They are very clever and much addicted to collecting shiny objects."

Well, what do you know about that?

I decided that I needed to get a closer look at this bird, so I strolled over to the tree. Sure enough, about twenty feet over my head was that pile of twigs—which I guessed was the bird's nest—and I could clearly see all sorts of bangles and gewgaws hanging from it.

There was nothing for it but to see if I could reach the nest.

It was one of those big, ancient massive trees—an oak or some such thing—that has branches sticking out all over it starting from just a few feet above the ground. It was kind of like the jungle gyms I used play around on when I was a kid. I'm not cut out for Tarzan stuff, but it was really like climbing a ladder. When I got to the right branch, I crawled out along it ten or twelve feet. I glanced down and saw that I was no longer twenty feet off the ground—I was now more than thirty feet over the road below. It was no good being bothered by that, so instead I looked at what lay just ahead of me and saw that I had been right. The nest was overflowing with necklaces, wrist-watches and all sorts of other whatnots. I straddled the branch and edged my way toward the nest. The branch was overhanging the road below and an occasional car or truck would zoom by, and I wondered what the drivers would have thought if they had bothered to look up as they passed by the tree.

When I reached the nest, I saw right away who the thief had been. The thing was filled with jewelry and watches and all sorts of other glittery what-nots.

I started poking around in the mess—there was my little chain and charm!—when something stabbed me in the back of the neck. I swatted at it, thinking it was a bee or a wasp or something, but it was the stupid bird. It was screeching and squawking and batting its wings in my face all the while apparently trying to peck my eyes out.

I yelled and swatted at it, but that just seemed to make it angrier. In trying to keep its beak and talons out of my face, I must have forgotten for a moment where I was. The bird took a dive at me, aiming its razor-sharp beak directly between my eyes, I raised my hands to fend it off and the next thing I knew I was tumbling through the air, with nothing below me but two lanes of asphalt.

Fortunately, a truck carrying a load of mattresses was passing by at that very moment and I fell into the back of it.

Unfortunately, the truck was making a non-stop run to Macy's.

✗

Ron Miller is an author/illustrator specializing in science, science fiction, and fantasy. He is responsible for 73 books of his own, many of which have received awards and commendations, including a Hugo. He has designed postage stamps (one of which is attached to the New Horizons spacecraft) and worked on motion pictures such as *Dune*.

www.ingramcontent.com/pod-product-compliance
Lightning Source LLC
Chambersburg PA
CBHW011448170626
46816CB00008B/2581